Teaching Can Be Murder

Jane DiLucchio
Quest Books
by Regal Crest

Tennessee

D1529488

ISBN 978-1-61929-262-8

First Printing 2015

9 8 7 6 5 4 3 2 1

Original cover design by AcornGraphics

Published by:

Regal Crest Enterprises
1042 Mount Lebanon Road
Maryville, TN 37804

Find us on the World Wide Web at
http://www.regalcrest.biz

Published in the United States of America

Acknowledgments

Thanks go to:

Jean Scott, Maureen McLaughlin and Sue Stimpson, patient beta readers extraordinaire;

Lynda Daniels, member of the Montrose Search and Rescue team, for her technical advice;

Heather Flournoy, for excellence in editing and for dedication to meeting deadlines despite overwhelming obstacles;

The Regal Crest publishing house for giving me a home;

My mother and sister for their encouragement;

Serra's Sisters, for supporting and loving me throughout this whole adventure.

Dedication

To Sue Stimpson, whose love and support give me the freedom to create.

Prologue

EARLY MORNING SUNLIGHT cast horizontal stripes across the floor of the elementary school classroom as it passed through the cracks of the Venetian blinds that covered four banks of windows. Dust danced in the beams of light before settling onto laminated wood desks, which had served hundreds of children. The desktops hid books, papers, gum, notes, and illicit materials which generations of students tried to keep from the notice of the teacher.

Hearts, flowers, and little cupids trimmed the bulletin boards of the room which were covered with children's writing samples and artwork. A fish tank burbled quietly on a side table while the three goldfish within drifted listlessly from side to side. The whiteboards were clean and clear, awaiting the lessons of the day.

Room Seven was ready for its teacher and fourth graders. Neat and clean—a testament to the diligence of the custodial staff of the Glendale Unified School District. Almost everything was in perfect order for another day of school.

The one discordant note was a red, sticky substance on the otherwise immaculate linoleum floor. A substance that had oozed from the back of the man lying prone in the aisle between the desks.

Chapter One

DIEGA DELVALLE JUGGLED her precariously balanced stack of papers and books in her right arm as she searched her purse for her room key. She shoved the errant key into the lock of her classroom at Vista Elementary School and swung the door wide.

Diega flipped on the light switch with her arm and plopped her papers and purse on her well-worn wooden desk. She brushed her wavy brown hair out of her eyes with her fingers, vowing to herself once again to call her friend Felicia for a haircut.

She walked to the windows and opened the Venetian blinds. The ancient, but still quite functional, grey steel coverings let in the morning sun. Although the sun felt warm through the windows, Diega knew better than to open them yet. The heated classroom air added to the illusion that the Southern California winter morning was as warm as it appeared.

Diega glanced at the clock, pleased that it was only 7:40. She liked to get to school a little earlier than most of the faculty. She wanted her classroom neat and organized so that both she and the students had a smooth start to their day.

Diega placed her purse in the bottom desk drawer. She grabbed the pole hook from the corner and opened the hallway transom windows over each door to get the air circulating in the room.

Taking out a red dry erase marker, she wrote "Wednesday, February 5, 1998" on the whiteboard. Pausing, she realized that Valentine's Day was a little over a week away, and for the first time in many years she would be celebrating alone. No expectations. No pressures. A pleasant feeling of relief infused her.

Refocusing, Diega wrote the reading group assignments on the board clearly and carefully. As always, she thought of Mr. Lee, her junior high school English teacher, who would line the chalkboard and write with the most precise handwriting Diega had ever seen outside of the handwriting samples in the spelling books. Although Diega could not emulate Mr. Lee's execution perfectly, she strove to have her writing be a good model for her students. Handwriting, she knew, was a dying art. But she was determined not to contribute to its extinction.

Diega finished the details of the Rockets reading group assignment and capped the pen. She was headed to the back cabinets to grab some fraction blocks for the math lesson when she noticed that the Petri dishes on the science center were out of place. Instead of being aligned in their labeled spots, it looked as though someone had shoved them to the back of the shelf. She switched paths to straighten them and stepped in a small, unidentifiable puddle.

Diega frowned as she pulled her foot up and back. Well conversant with the vagaries of bodily fluids children seem inclined to share with the world, she hopped carefully to the classroom sink and turned on the tap. No water trickled forth. Only then did she remember that her room had a leak the previous day. Obviously Facilities and Maintenance was not as efficient as the custodians. She grabbed a paper towel instead.

Before she could wipe the mess from her shoe, Diega heard heavy breathing behind her. Given that no teachers she knew jogged to school, she felt a bit perplexed.

Diega's surprise grew when she turned to face Rita Morgan. Rita taught next door to Diega. In this case, proximity bred near contempt. Diega tried at all costs to avoid Rita and Rita returned the favor. Thus the sight of the dark-haired Rita at her door was startling enough. But Rita was also pale beneath her blush—so pale her blue eye shadow seemed to make her eyes bulge.

Diega took note of all of this in fewer seconds than it took for Rita to hyperventilate once more, point down the hall, and gasp, "He's... room..."

Diega poked her head into the hallway in the direction of Rita's wavering, French-tipped, pink fingernail. She inched down the hall, conscious of the snicking noise her shoe made as it stuck to the waxed hallway with each step. She paused outside of Rita's classroom door and listened.

No irate voices.

No stomping or tossing of inanimate objects.

Diega glanced over her shoulder at Rita, who was now collapsed against the doorjamb, sobbing. Shrugging, Diega looked inside classroom number seven. Her glance did not have very far to travel before it spotted a man in a grey, pinstriped business suit lying face down on the floor. Face down and very dead.

"DIEGA DELVALLE," DIEGA said, in answer to the third police officer to question her, this one a short, broad-shouldered detective with a prominent nose. She thought it was strange how few people ever pronounced her name correctly, even in the heavily Hispanic culture that was Los Angeles. Of course, Diega mused, Glendale was now heavily leaning in the direction of an Armenian population. Diega caught her thoughts drifting and realized she had not heard the detective's last question.

"You say you know the victim?" the detective asked again.

Diega focused this time, remembering the detective's name was Gregory Theophilus. A Greek in the midst of Glendale. The world was indeed shrinking, she thought as she said aloud, "Yes. Zeke Chambers." She paused and looked into the dark eyes of the Glendale police detective. "It was Zeke, wasn't it?"

The detective laid his notebook on his lap. "It seems so. The I.D. in his wallet bears that name. So tell me again how you knew Mr. Chambers."

Diega related yet again that Zeke Chambers was the assistant superintendent in charge of special projects for the Glendale Unified School District, and how the two of them worked on the same committee for a school improvement project. "We also see each other during negotiations. Opposite sides of the table, but we sometimes confer." That the conferring lately had taken place over a glass of wine, Diega left out.

Diega sat back in the plastic chair awaiting the next round of questions. The teacher's lounge had been transformed into an impromptu interrogation room after school had been abruptly cancelled for the day. Students who had already arrived had been herded into the auditorium to await custodial transportation back home. Diega imagined most parents would be none too pleased with this unanticipated school holiday.

"What did Mr. Chambers do for the district?"

"Just what his title implies. He was in charge of any projects that were above and beyond the normal running of the schools."

"And that meant he did what exactly?" Detective Theophilus's body seemed relaxed, but his dark eyes never left her face.

"I'm really not sure all of what his job entailed. You'd have to ask the superintendent."

Theophilus nodded his head and consulted his book again. "Did Mr. Chambers visit Vista Elementary very often?"

Diega reached forward and grabbed her blue mug that bore the sentiments, "Don't Let the Turkeys Get You Down." She sipped the coffee as she considered her answer. Swallowing, she said, "I've seen him here occasionally before this year, but he's been here more often since September."

"To visit you?"

Diega tried to compose her features. Bluffing had never been her strong suit. In fact, her Uncle Juan, a renowned poker expert, had once advised her to stay away from gambling at all costs. "One look at your face, *mi hija*, and they'll not only know what's in your hand, but what you're planning on confessing in church on Sunday."

Diega kept her voice neutral. "Zeke never visited me here."

Theophilus let the silence linger before changing topics. "How would you characterize your relationship with the victim?"

"Friendly. But we didn't play on the same field."

When the detective cocked an eyebrow, Diega elaborated. "Zeke was a main office administrator. I'm a classroom teacher. I liked Zeke." She stopped and swallowed, afraid that tears would flow. A deep breath later she said, "I appreciated the changes he was trying to make, the improvements he was trying to institute. I happen to think he was one of the good guys in the district. But we were not social."

Detective Theophilus took his time flipping through his notebook. Diega remained quiet, even stifling the urge to scratch her neck. She realized she was trying to draw as little attention to herself as possible.

After several moments the detective stared into her eyes yet again. "Let me review. You say you arrived here at approximately 7:35 a.m. You saw 'a few' cars in the parking lot, but you don't remember which cars or where they were. You walked straight to your room, Room Five, and did not notice anyone else in the hallway. And you heard no unusual noises. Is that accurate?"

Diega held up a finger. "About the cars. I don't know if it helps or not, but I know for sure that there wasn't one on either side of me. I had to open both side doors to unload some folders and I remember thinking I was glad I didn't have to worry about scratching a neighboring car."

The detective looked at a sketch of the parking lot and then down at a list of names. "So those would be the spaces assigned to Ms. Rita Morgan in Room Seven and Ms. Lorraine Haley in Room Three."

"That's right. Lorraine doesn't usually come in early. She's been teaching thirty years. Good teacher. Has the whole thing down pat so she doesn't need much prep time. Rita's also been around a while, but she still comes early occasionally. She sometimes parks her car on the side street. It's nearer her room. When we have a lot to carry, being only a few steps closer can help." Diega realized she was rambling and clamped her jaws shut.

Detective Theophilus did not react to her sudden garrulousness any more than he had her shorter answers. He only made more notes on his pad. "Do you have anything else to add to your statement at this time?"

Diega sat back and visualized her arrival that morning. Had she known that it would be important, perhaps she would have paid more attention. But nothing on the radio, nothing in the blue skies, nothing in the raucous wild parrot calls that were becoming more common in the San Fernando Valley, nothing had given her warning that this morning would be different from every other school day of her last fourteen years of teaching.

"I can't think of anything right now. But you'll be the first to know if something comes up."

Detective Theophilus closed his notebook and handed her his card. "I'd sure appreciate it."

As Diega rose, the detective cleared his throat.

"One other thing," he said, pointing at Diega's feet. "We need your shoes."

Chapter Two

"SO THE GREEK has a shoe fetish?" Tallulah Bouchart, Tully to her friends, leaned her voluptuous frame forward and grabbed another oatmeal cookie from the platter on Diega's burl wood coffee table. "Seems like he shouldn't be able to indulge that on taxpayer's time."

Predictably, Tully had already left four phone messages for Diega before Diega had even made the fifteen-minute drive home from Glendale to Burbank that afternoon. The news had hit the media and Tully had hit the telephone buttons. Each of Tully's successive messages increased in frustration. It appalled Tully that Diega refused to carry her newly-acquired cell phone with her to school, and today's events made that evident.

Diega had barely dumped her school bags in the room she reserved as her office and creative arts space when the doorbell rang. All five feet ten inches of her best friend crammed Diega's doorway. Coerced into parting with all the gory details, Diega filled her friend in as she changed out of her slacks, blouse, and socks and into jeans, T-shirt and mercifully bare feet. Diega had never figured out how women had been convinced that high heels were a necessary part of adult life, so she did not feel a desolate sense of loss over the short, black boots that the police had confiscated.

"I don't know why they wanted my shoes. That goo I stepped in must have left footprints in Rita's room. Or maybe I tracked through the blood on the floor, except I don't remember getting that close to Zeke's body."

Tully stretched and lifted her currently brown, shoulder length hair off her neck. Tully changed hair color like some people changed bed sheets—almost weekly, whether they needed it or not. "Isn't this Zeke the guy who's been feeding you info on negotiations?"

Diega served on the teacher's union negotiating team. The current round of negotiations had been extremely frustrating with the school district balking on healthcare issues while insisting on budget cuts. State funding had taken a downward turn once again, causing friction over appropriations, priorities, and core values among teachers, administration, and the classified staff.

Diega flexed her toes as she thought about all that she had not told the detective about Zeke Chambers. "If it wasn't for Zeke, I wouldn't have known about the real numbers behind the healthcare rebates that the district gets. I wouldn't know about the huge waste in administration with the duplication of duties. He gave me ammunition. We're going to bust open negotiations because of him." She felt the anger and sadness vying for prominence within her. "I owe him. Big time."

Tully pushed the tray of oatmeal cookies closer to Diega. "I think your blood sugar needs a boost. You're not usually so emotional over union issues." She leaned back again and gazed at Diega. "You didn't tell the good detective about your little extra-curricular pow-wows with Zeke, did you?"

"No way. Can you imagine the fallout? The union would have to throw me off the team." Diega grew somber. "Rightfully so. I still don't know why I agreed to talk with him."

"'Cause you were losing and you hate to lose."

"Maybe." Diega squeezed her eyes shut, but the image of Zeke's bloody body appeared. Her eyes flew open. "It was horrible, Tully. No one deserves what happened to Zeke. I don't know why I feel responsible, but I do." A sudden thought amplified her guilt. "You don't think someone in the administration found out about Zeke talking to me and decided to stop him, do you?"

"I know you aren't particularly fond of the district honchos, but murder is a little extreme for a termination policy, even for the heartless, soulless entities who dare to work in administration."

"I still feel like I should do something."

Tully breathed a sigh that lasted almost as long as their decade of friendship. "Now, Dee, hold your little doggies. We all know how you can get on your crusades and go marching off to right some wrong."

"Like Don Quixote, but with boobs?"

"Something like that." Tully flashed a grin. "Come to think of it, you do have the olive skin and dark hair, but I don't recall that the Don had hazel eyes or a cute little nose, but, hey, it's your metaphor, not mine."

"Simile," Diega said as she reached for a cookie. "A metaphor is a direct comparison."

"You teachers are a pain in the ass."

"Now, that," Diega said, "is a metaphor."

Tully ignored her. "Have you seen the news coverage?" she asked as she swiped the last cookie from the plate. "You sure could tell that Glendale is right close to Burbank and all our attendant news studios."

"I had to sneak out the back door and have Jim drive my car around to meet me. I couldn't face the rather dense crowd of reporters in front of the school."

"Might have been hard to explain your stocking feet," Tully said, nodding at Diega freed toes. "Maybe you could have convinced them it's the new dress code for teachers." She slapped her thighs. "Since you were not the victim and I don't have to bail you out of jail this time, my job here is done."

"You've never had to bail me out of jail."

"Fine, Ms. Stickler-For-Details. Unlike with your paramour's untimely death, this time I did not have to track down a defense lawyer to save your lovely ass from jail until our unparalleled detection skills uncovered the real murderer."

Diega snorted. "Detection skills? Dumb luck is more like it. Besides, that fabulous defense lawyer you hired then stole my girlfriend."

Tully tutted. "Now who's blurring the details? As I recall, your fling with the late unlamented had already, pardon the term, killed your relationship with Evie. Our legal eagle Marsha just swooped in and grabbed our sweet little Evie, easy prey that she was." She rose. "So much for wandering down the lovely memory lane of past murder pursuits. I've got to run."

"Hot Wednesday night date?"

Tully waggled her eyebrows. "As a matter of fact..." She whacked Diega's shoulder. "Hey, why don't you come along?"

"Somehow I'm not quite in the party mood."

"Brooding is not allowed." Tully kicked the side of Diega's seat. "So drag your sorry butt out of the chair and come with us. It'll be kind of a double date without the bother of person number four. Unless you want to call on one of your new lovelies."

Diega shook her head. "No thanks. After today, I'd like to stay home, pet the cats, have a drink, watch TV, have another drink, and forget about interacting with people."

"Someday, my friend, you are going to learn that life is short and you have to enjoy every blessed second." Tully shook her head. "But I guess I won't physically drag you out of your shell tonight."

Diega flipped on the local news as Tully gathered her jacket and camera. A freelance entertainment photographer by trade, Tully rarely travelled anywhere without her trusty lenses.

A scene on the television of the faux Spanish-style exterior of Vista Elementary caught Diega's eye. Increasing the volume via remote, Diega heard the on-the-spot reporter say, "The police will be holding a news conference tomorrow morning. Although no arrests have yet been made, unnamed sources confirm that the police have strong evidence linking one of the school employees to the scene of the crime."

Diega looked down at her shoeless feet and then at Tully. "Son of a bitch."

Chapter Three

THE NEXT MORNING, as Diega read the rather sensationalized version of events that the Los Angeles Times printed, she found herself feeling sorry for Zeke Chambers's family. She felt they should hear the truth. She grabbed the phone and awoke Tully, who groggily agreed to accompany her to Zeke's home after school.

The grey, asphalt parking lot was sparsely occupied at seven-thirty when Diega pulled her trusty purple Hyundai into space number five. This morning she took note of the other early arrivals. Steve Johnson had his ancient, brown pickup truck tucked into space number two. Two newer-model, grey cars were parked side-by-side in spaces eight and ten, meaning Gail Landers and Lilith Abramian had both arrived. Sally Nelson, the new principal, had her forest green Audi parked in her zoned slot by the front of the building. A police car and an old sedan were parked along the curb.

Diega wondered about Zeke Chambers's car. She did not know what kind of car Zeke drove, and she paid little attention to cars anyway, so the likelihood that she would have consciously or unconsciously noticed anything different in the parking lot was small. But she forced herself to think about the lot yesterday. Was there a different car in here, or had Zeke parked on the street? Street parking was tight on Wednesdays since it was street-sweeping day, but early in the morning that restriction would not have mattered very much. She squeezed her eyes shut in an attempted visualization of the parking lot that day.

"Closing your eyes and pretending won't make it go away." Jim Tolkien's voice jolted Diega back to the reality of Vista Elementary and the teaching day ahead.

Diega smiled at the sight of her teaching partner. Although over a decade too late for the sixties, Jim always saw himself as a member of that generation. His long, greying hair, tied back in a ponytail, made that claim somewhat believable. "Clicking my heels was next, but you interrupted me before I could get back to Oz." Diega pulled her bag higher on her shoulder and walked with him up the ramp leading to the side entrance of the school.

Jim Tolkien had been Diega's assigned mentor when she first started teaching at Vista. It was thanks to this quiet, pudgy rebel that Diega had become involved in the teachers' union and now served with him on the negotiating team.

In a gentlemanly gesture, Jim unlocked the side door and waved Diega inside. The hallways were clean, with no signs of forensic work or crime scene tape.

"I wonder where Rita is going to hold her class?" Diega said as she and Jim turned to the right and headed down the light blue hallway to their rooms. "I imagine Room Seven is still off limits."

They stopped in front of Room One, or, as Jim liked to refer to it, his "Palace of Insurrection." He delighted in exposing fifth graders to a wider world than many of their parents—or the school district—might believe prudent. Any topic that touched the heart of this aging hippie was somehow integrated into the approved curriculum with little or no outcry from the administration or parents.

"I heard they pulled in a bungalow overnight. It might mean you'll have no neighbor to annoy for the rest of the semester."

Diega hitched the strap of her bag up again. "Gee, Rita gone out of my life. How could I be so lucky?"

Jim put a finger to his lips. "You may want to watch what you say, at least until this thing fades away. Some people may not understand your sense of humor."

Chastised, Diega walked silently to her room. She was puzzled, then furious to see a crime scene tape crisscrossed over her door. Shoving her books up higher in her arms, she stomped down the hall to the principal's office.

"Sally," Diega said, as she marched past the school secretary and through the principal's open door. "What the hell—"

Diega clipped her remarks at the sight of Detective Theophilus lounging in a chair beside Sally Nelson's empty desk.

"Ms. DelValle," he said with a wave of his hand indicating a vacant guest chair. "I was going to look you up in a few minutes."

"Didn't you get enough of me yesterday? Should I pencil you in for the rest of the week?" Diega gave him a glare that wilted the most obstinate fourth grader. Theophilus, however, appeared unfazed. "Look, I have a class that starts in forty-five minutes and I have a boarded-up classroom. Any suggestions as to what I should do with my twenty-eight little cherubs when they arrive in the next half hour or so?"

Theophilus grinned. "I haven't figured out what to do with one ten-year-old and one seven-year-old. I couldn't imagine dealing with scores of them."

Diega raised an eyebrow and sat down in the empty chair. "A sense of humor. Not quite what I'd expect from a homicide detective."

"A raging temper. Not what I'd expect from an elementary school teacher."

Diega's reply was interrupted by a blur of blue silk swishing by. Sally Nelson, blond hair professionally colored and faultlessly styled, slipped into her leather chair. The principal's hair might have been perfect, but Diega noticed that her deep-set eyes were ringed with a fatigue that even her expert makeup could not conceal. Sally picked up a keen-edged silver letter opener and started bouncing it on her desk.

This was the first time Diega had seen the unflappable woman show any signs of stress. It made her more human, but Diega was unwilling to think that it made her any more likeable.

The principal laid the letter opener aside and intertwined her fingers. "Diega, your class has been moved into the auditorium for today. I thought the police would be finished with your classroom by now, but Detective Theophilus feels they need more time." She gave the detective a glance then swung her attention back to Diega. "Luis is setting up chairs and tables. Since we can't get anything out of your classroom, I've arranged for a set of textbooks to be delivered from the district office, but I don't know when they will arrive. However, you'll have a portable whiteboard and paper and pencils. Since you don't bother to follow the curriculum anyway, I'm sure you'll make do."

A rap on the doorframe made all three of the room's occupants swivel in their seats. The powerfully built body of Patrick Nelson, the principal's husband, filled the doorway. Diega had met him at a faculty party when Sally had first arrived and she had been impressed by his warmth and humor. What this gentle contractor saw in the cold, formal Sally, Diega could not fathom, but there were odder couples in the world.

Patrick was tall and broad with thinning auburn hair combed carefully over a balding spot on the back of his head. He wore a white dress shirt with the sleeves rolled up. Gashes and old bruises marred his muscular arms, leading Diega to believe that he not only owned his business, but spent time on the building sites with tools in hand. Diega noticed two fresh bandages on his right forearm and knuckles. The sight made her proud that she had fought for spousal health insurance coverage from the district.

Patrick glanced at the others in the room before addressing his wife. "Sorry to interrupt, but I brought you a surprise."

A young woman slipped into the room. She was of medium build, but fit and tanned, the kind of tan one gets from outdoor living rather than a tanning booth. Chin-length, wavy, strawberry blond hair framed a face, which bore a half smile.

"Sorry to break in on your meeting," she said. Before she could say anything else, Sally swept from behind her desk and encased her in a hug.

"Your hair," Sally said, running her fingers alongside the other's face.

"What? You miss the curls?"

The only response was another hug.

Diega glanced at Theophilus, who looked equally interested in the loving exchange occurring four feet away. Diega was trying to fit this emotional display into her mental picture of her iceberg principal when Sally turned to them, wiping her eyes.

"I'm sorry. It's just that I haven't seen her in almost three months." She teared up again.

"Since my mom seems uncharacteristically incoherent, let me do the honors. I'm Erin Nelson." She stuck out her hand to Diega and then to the detective.

Diega could see the family resemblance. In many ways Sally's daughter was a thirty-something, physically stronger version of her. Both blond, although Erin's had a reddish tinge, perhaps, Diega thought, a testament to her father's DNA. Both blue-eyed, although Diega thought Erin's eyes were on the icier side whereas her mother's were a deep, rich blue. Erin was a little shorter than her mother, bringing her about equal in height to Diega.

Diega watched the family reunion with some puzzlement. She could see her own mother making a big deal of her homecoming, but this display of maternal outpouring by Sally seemed extreme. It added to Diega's puzzlement when she noticed that Patrick had backed away from the two women and was standing, legs spread, hands shoved in his pockets.

As intriguing as the dynamic was, Diega's inner alarm clock was telling her that students were moments away from her makeshift classroom. She looked at the detective. "I'm afraid we'll have to have our chat later." She excused herself to the others and made her way to the auditorium.

Diega sighed at the hodge-podge of hastily assembled furniture. Obviously, Luis, the school's custodian, had dragged out every desk that had ever been stuffed into the basement of the school. Mismatched was an understatement. She thought she could recognize at least five decades of desk and chair styles arranged in rows on the auditorium stage. Staring at the board, it dawned on her that she did not have her lesson plans, her teacher's editions of the texts, or any teaching materials.

However, rather than the practicalities of planning how to survive the day, Diega found her thoughts drifting to Sally Nelson's family. Why the reunion in Sally's office rather than at home? Why did Sally seem so concerned about her daughter? And why did Sally's husband hold himself back?

And what did Detective Theophilus want with her now?

Chapter Four

"YOU SURE YOU want to do this?" Tully yawned as Diega pulled up to the curb in front of the brightly painted blue and yellow sign of the Friendly Florist shop on Verdugo Road in Glendale. Tully gulped the last swallow of her hazelnut coffee in what Diega could only imagine as an attempt to fully awaken. It appeared to have only a limited effect.

"Late date night, huh?" Diega patted her friend on the arm. "As for wanting to do this, no. But it's the right thing to do. You don't have to come in with me."

"Here or at the Widow Chambers's house?"

"Either one." Diega slipped out the driver's side and walked quickly into the shop. She returned in less than ten minutes carrying a white wicker basket containing a blooming pink azalea plant. She deposited it on the back seat.

Diega guided her metallic purple Hyundai up the curving road until reaching a small side street about a mile into the hilly area of Glendale known as the Verdugo Woodlands. She parked in front of a monumental Spanish two-story house with a red tile roof and white, plastered adobe walls.

"Hard to believe, but this is it," Diega said as she double-checked the piece of paper on which she had written Zeke Chambers's home address.

The front door was hidden behind a thick adobe wall that stretched the length of the front yard. A stamped concrete path bisected the sloping, deep green front lawn and led to a wide wooden door set in an arched doorway in the wall.

"Not exactly a welcome mat is it?" Tully said as they stared at the dark wooden door crossed with studs and attached to the wall with black iron hinges.

"There doesn't seem to be a doorbell. Do we simply walk in?"

Tully reached for the black iron latch, which opened under her touch.

Inside the gate was a courtyard lined with potted plants. A brick path meandered up to the double wooden front door. Climbing yellow roses provided shade along each side of the doors.

Tully raised an eyebrow. "You sure you work in the same place this guy did?"

"The district office must pay a lot better than I thought. Maybe the union needs to check into that."

The door was opened by a muscular, unshaven teenager with a newly-sprouted mustache and a sullen look on his face. His biceps showed signs of time at the gym and he emphasized that part of his build by wearing a tight, white T-shirt. Both his hands were wrapped as if he had recently returned from a boxing match. He was wearing deep blue sweatpants. Dark, unwelcoming eyes surveyed the women, but he did not speak.

"I'm Diega DelValle and this is my friend Tallulah Bouchart. I worked with your father. I wanted to come by and give your family my condolences."

The boy's face was impassive during Diega's recital. At first she thought he would refuse them entrance, but he stood aside and jerked his head toward the right of the entryway.

He led them to a living room that could, in Diega's estimation, have doubled for a reception hall. Enormous arched, beveled windows lit the vast expanse of wooden floor that stretched across the room. A stone fireplace that could have roasted a whole pig occupied the center of the interior wall. Dark wooden beams held the ceiling in place.

"Mom," the young man yelled in the direction of the stairway to the right of the room. "Visitors." His duty obviously done in his mind, he left the two women standing in the middle of the room.

A tall, slender woman descended the staircase with an elegance that Diega always associated with money. The woman wore black slacks and a black silk blouse with a black and white scarf around her shoulders. She had raven-black hair and dark eyes that contrasted with her pale skin. Her eyes were puffy, but her makeup disguised any other signs of grief.

Diega repeated her introductions and handed the woman the plant. Mrs. Chambers waved them to seats on the oversized couch opposite the fireplace.

Diega cleared her throat. "I didn't know your husband very well, but since I was the one who...found him, I feel connected in a way."

Mrs. Chambers nodded her head. "I see." Her voice was low and melodic. "Zeke didn't talk much about his work, so I'm afraid I don't know many of his co-workers. Were you here for the district office Christmas party? I'm sorry for not recognizing you. There were so many people that I find I don't remember many of them. You know how large parties can become a blur."

Diega nodded without clarifying her lack of attendance at any parties here, large or small. "Do you need any help notifying people at the district concerning any services?"

Mrs. Chambers shook her head. "My secretary is taking care of all that, but I do appreciate your offer, Ms. DelValle."

"Call me Diega."

"Then you must call me Noelle."

Since Diega did not remember calling her by any name, she chalked it up to good manners.

"I'm getting the hell out of here." The teen who had answered the door appeared briefly. He had changed out of his gym clothes and into jeans and a yellow polo shirt. He had a brown leather jacket slung over his arm. He barely glanced at his mother before shooting through the front door and slamming it behind him. The revving of a motor loud enough to indicate that the motorcycle was in dire need of a muffler followed shortly after his exit.

"Please forgive Wayne. He has been extremely upset by his father's death."

Diega doubted that, but did not want to raise that issue right now. "I was wondering if you knew why your husband was at the school that morning. I only ask because I hadn't seen him in my wing of the building before then, and I wondered if he was coming to see me."

Noelle's face grew impassive. "How exactly did you know my husband?"

"We both served on the negotiations teams for the district." Diega deliberately left it vague as to which side she was on.

Noelle seemed to relax. "Perhaps he was trying to find you. I know he has...had...negotiations next week. He was also working on a project with the principal at your school. Perhaps he was hunting her down. Whatever he was doing there, I only wish he hadn't gone. Otherwise he would still be here." She looked off into the distance. The chimes of the grandfather clock in the corner seemed to recall her to the room. "I'm afraid I have an appointment with the funeral home. But thank you so much for coming by."

She escorted them to the front door and closed it firmly behind them.

Tully looked at Diega. "Sonny boy's not too broken up, is he?"

"Sure doesn't seem that way."

As they climbed into Diega's car, the electric gate on the Chambers's driveway slid back and a black Porsche with Mrs. Chambers at the wheel glided onto the street. Before she could pull away, a midnight blue Harley roared up beside her. The helmeted driver held a quick conversation with Noelle Chambers who then rolled up the window of the Porsche and drove away. The Harley driver flipped up his facemask revealing the scowling face of Zeke's son. He glared at his mother's car and lifted a middle finger to her in salute.

Chapter Five

DIEGA'S CATS, BB and Sherwood Forrest, wound pleadingly around her legs as she made her way to the back door from her garage. Obviously happy to end their outside playtime in exchange for a meal, they raced through the cat door before Diega could even unlock the back door and step into the kitchen.

Beelzebub, BB for short, stridently proclaimed her state of starvation, while blinking green eyes that stood out from her thick black fur like two sunlit emeralds on a black velvet cloth. Knowing dinner had been delayed with her visit to the Chambers's household, Diega found her pathetic vocalizations hard to resist. Since this was true even on routine days, it explained her ever-rounding middle.

Sherwood, a hefty Maine Coon with long, luxuriant grey fur and blue eyes, was a bit more refined. She preferred to let BB do most of the begging, then take her own share of the rewards.

The telephone rang as Diega popped open the lid to a can that purported to hold filets of beef in gravy. She stuffed the receiver between her shoulder and ear as she tried to divide the brown shredded meat evenly between the two vocal cats.

Jenny Fenton's warm, low voice filled Diega's ear. "We know you've got all those wonderfully exciting things happening at work," she said, "but we were wondering if you could tear yourself away and join us for a party at Felicia's on Sunday afternoon."

Diega did not have to ask who the "we" was. Jenny had been dating Felicia Delacroix for almost a year. The two women, Tully, and Diega had been a platonic foursome for several years before Jenny and Felicia had admitted to a mutual attraction.

The two made a handsome contrast. Jenny, a public relations expert who was currently between jobs, was tall with wide shoulders and slim hips, long, wavy brown hair, and pale skin. Felicia, a stylist and makeup artist for a local television news show, was shorter and stockier with short, curly black hair and beautiful, smooth cafe-au-lait skin. Merely thinking of the two of them together made Diega smile.

"Normally that would sound like a lot of fun," Diega said, "but, honestly, I don't know about a big party. Zeke's death has hit me harder than I would have thought."

"That's because you've always been a lot more sensitive than you ever care to admit." Jenny paused. "Look, there's no better way to distract yourself than by partying. You can even bring one of your multiple trial girlfriends along."

"Good grief. You really don't believe me that I'm happy by myself. You guys jump on me if I sit at home—comfortably, I might add—or if I go out with someone new and find out I'm not interested. I can't win."

Jenny sighed, conveying more worry than frustration. "Fine. Don't bring a date. But regardless of your mood, you have to come. This isn't just a party. I'm not saying anything more, but you have to be here."

Diega finally agreed. She reluctantly gave up her fantasy of sitting contentedly by the fire with the cats, a book, and a glass of wine on a cool Southern California winter afternoon and substituted an image of being in the midst of a swarm of people. She knew Tully would delight in such an event, finding the possibilities of meeting multiple new women too tempting to miss. Personally, she found the idea exhausting.

"By the way," Diega added, "how's the job hunting coming?"

Jenny's voice grew more animated. "I heard back from the LAPD, I've got a second interview for the public information office position."

"Quite a switch from P.R. for the hospital."

"Yes and no. I worked with the police a lot on what information should and should not be released in several criminal cases. That's how I met Ray."

Diega knew Ray was a senior officer on the force and that he had been the one to suggest Jenny apply for the opening. "No problem with the whole transgender issue?"

"They've done a background check. They know very well I was born Jimmy Fenton. Nobody has brought it up."

"Who knew the homophobic culture of the LAPD could be so progressive?" Diega considered the advances she had witnessed over the last decade and conceded that the department may, indeed, be evolving. "We should include a toast to your future with the newly open-minded police department at the party."

"If that's what it takes to get you there, I'll personally chill the Champagne."

After bidding Jenny adieu, Diega scooped up the already empty cat dishes and dumped them in the sink. Some of the remnants of the meal stuck on her thumb. She fingered the sticky glop of brown gravy and thought of the unidentified puddle in her classroom that she had stepped in on Wednesday.

Diega grabbed a brown pair of short boots out of her bedroom. She made sure the soles were similar to the ones she had worn Friday. She lifted the cat food dishes out of the sink and scraped the remaining bit of leftover sauce from each onto the kitchen floor. Then she placed the heel of the boot on the puddle. It stuck slightly in a manner reminiscent of the liquid in her classroom.

Diega sat on the floor beside the brown muck and contemplated her experiment. How would gravy get on the floor of her classroom? Students did not eat lunch in the room unless it was a rainy day and it had been a very dry winter.

Simulating walking, Diega pressed the heel of the boot to the floor. There was the same sticking sensation she remembered when she walked down the hallway to Room Seven.

"Curiouser and curiouser," Diega said to BB who had come over to do her own investigating.

After sniffing Diega's boot and the kitchen floor, BB flicked her tail and walked away disdainfully. Diega grabbed a sponge and cleaned away her foray into forensics.

FRIDAY FEATURED DIEGA'S return to her real classroom. She made a quick inspection of her space to ensure that all evidence of police activity had been erased. The efficiency of the custodial staff was once again in evidence. Satisfied, Diega sat at her wide, wooden desk and started sorting through her hasty notes of the previous day.

A cross between a cough and a growl came from the doorway. Detective Theophilus waved when Diega swiveled to face him.

"We should be finished with the room next door in a couple of days," he said, shoving his hands in his pockets and rocking back on his heels. His gaze toured the walls before returning to Diega's face. "I'm sure you're happy to be back in your own room."

"Ecstatic," Diega said, unsure why he provoked nasty responses from her.

He nodded, as if she had uttered a profoundly philosophical thought. He crossed his arms and leaned against the doorjamb. "We never got to have our chat yesterday. I need to clear up a couple of things. You said you didn't mingle with Mr. Chambers, isn't that right?"

Diega nodded.

"Yet you and he were seen at a restaurant in Burbank one week ago. The two of you. Alone." He raised an eyebrow.

Diega reddened and sank back into her desk chair. "Zeke served on the district's side of the negotiating team. I serve on the union side. Generally speaking, those sides are not best friends."

The detective did not move, obviously waiting for Diega to continue.

"The district's team had refuted our offer using faulty numbers. Since that's my area, I confronted Zeke. He wanted a chance to explain." She shrugged. "I gave him a chance."

"The report suggested something a little cozier than a chat about numbers."

"Then I would wonder about the quality of the reports you're receiving. Zeke and I talked about negotiations. Something that will get me thrown off the team if it becomes widely known. So I didn't want to mention it."

"Would Mr. Chambers have had any problems because of talking with you?"

Diega snorted. "Quite a few. At the very least he'd be exiled from the district's negotiating team. He'd probably be chewed out by the superintendent and maybe even reprimanded by the Board. For sure they'd never trust him again."

The detective thumbed through his notebook then stared at Diega. "Kinda makes you wonder why he'd do that." He shrugged and slipped his notebook into his jacket pocket. "Have you have ever given your room key to anyone?"

Diega leaned forward in her chair. "Are you asking if I've ever given anyone a copy? If so, cross that off your list. The key has a big 'Do Not Duplicate' stamped on it."

"I've never known that to deter burglars." Before Diega could object, Theophilus continued, "I'm more interested to know if anyone has ever asked to borrow your key."

Diega looked out the classroom window and admired the lacy sunlight that filtered through the tiny leaves of the elm tree growing in the playground as she pondered. "I've given it to people sometimes, like when I'm outside and I need something from the classroom. But I don't remember anyone ever asking me if they could borrow it."

"When you gave out your key, would it be to students or to other teachers?"

"Both. It depends." Diega interrupted the flow. "Why are you so interested in my classroom?" She jerked her thumb in the direction of Room Seven. "Zeke was killed next door and my key doesn't fit any other room."

Theophilus did not respond. "Do you know anyone with a master key for the building?"

"I'm sure there's a list somewhere at the district office. If you're asking for my personal knowledge, I'd say our principal, Sally Nelson, and the custodians. I haven't seen any teachers flashing one around."

"How about Zeke Chambers?"

"How should I know? That's one for the district head honchos."

"Zeke was issued a master key for Vista Elementary."

Diega blew out air loudly. "Well, if you knew that, why ask me?"

"The funny thing is, Mr. Chambers did not have one on his person when he died." When Diega did not respond, Theophilus continued, "Did you hear or see Ms. Morgan on Wednesday morning before she came to your classroom?"

Diega flashed through her arrival and morning activities in her mind. She did not remember noticing anything about Rita Morgan that morning. Upon reflection it did seem strange that she had not heard stirrings through the wall. Rita's classroom was, after all, right next to hers. "I didn't see Rita arrive, but a lot of times she comes through the far entrance." Thinking about it, Diega realized that Rita was probably as happy to avoid running into her, as she was to avoid Rita. "I'm sure I must have heard her unlock her door, but it's a usual sound so I don't recall it registering, if you know what I mean."

Theophilus asked, "How long did it take you to find Mr. Chambers from the time Ms. Morgan appeared at your door?"

It was Diega's turn to become silent as she tried to replay those moments on the scene of her mind. "Fifteen, maybe thirty seconds. It took me maybe ten seconds to comprehend what Rita was saying and then another ten to creep down the hall to the far door of Rita's room. I didn't know what to expect and I wasn't in a hurry to face an irate parent who had sent Rita into shock."

"When you went into the room that morning, did you happen to pick up any object and maybe take it with you? You know how it is when you see something out of place and shove it in your pocket without really thinking about it."

"Not that I remember. Anything in particular that you're looking for? Are you thinking I pocketed his master key?"

The detective changed directions. "I understand you were involved in a murder investigation a couple of years ago."

"What's that got to do with anything?"

"I understand you were high on the suspect list initially. Why might someone think you capable of murder?"

At the moment Diega could gladly have killed whoever had been blabbing to the policeman, but decided that would be a counterproductive activity. "I imagine we're all capable of killing someone given the right motivation. Even you."

He smiled. "And yet they let me carry a gun. Careless of the department, don't you think?" His eyes returned to the notebook and he changed the course of the questioning yet again. "You said earlier that you did not touch the body. Is that still your recollection?"

"I took a step or two toward him. I can't say how close I got, but I didn't actually touch him."

"Why not?"

The detective's question made Diega consider her actions. "I don't really know. Partly because of the huge pair of scissors sticking out of his back. Partly the bloody mess. And partly...his eyes." She closed her own eyes tightly.

Silence from Theophilus caused Diega to explain further. "He was on his stomach with blood seeping from his back. His head was turned to the side, facing me. He had blood across his upper lip and mouth as well, like he was wearing a red mustache. His eyes were narrowed. He didn't look surprised. He looked pissed." Diega took a deep breath to try to rid her inner movie screen of that vision. She said forcefully, "He looked angry and he looked dead. Neither one made me want to get any closer."

Theophilus did not speak for several seconds. "Any idea how he got some of your hair in his hand?"

Chapter Six

DIEGA WAS STILL processing the departed detective's comments when Erin Nelson took his place in the doorframe.

"Have you seen my mom this morning?"

Diega's distracted, negative reply did not seem to motivate the principal's daughter to search elsewhere for her mother. Diega wanted time to think about all that Theophilus had said, but instead, she got an unwanted intruder wandering into the classroom who seemed in no hurry to leave.

Erin picked up one of the taxidermic animals lined up along the window. She hefted a bobcat. "I've run across these in the mountains. They're a lot prettier alive and in the wild."

"I have the school archivist's solemn guarantee," Diega said, "that all of these exhibits died a natural death."

Erin said to the bobcat, "Too bad you aren't alive. I bet you could sell that woman the Golden Gate Bridge." She picked up a Petri dish filled with fuzz. "What's this?"

"A science experiment. I got samples of fur from all the different mammals I could and put them in separate Petri dishes. Students are going to examine each under the microscope. They'll record differences, similarities, and see if they can match the mammal with its hair."

Diega watched Erin examine the display.

"So," Diega said, as much out of politeness as any sense of curiosity since the woman did not seem inclined to hurry to her mother's side, "you like to hike."

"Hike, boat, mountain bike. I just got back from skiing and rock climbing in the Alps. Scared me to death, but it was gorgeous."

"Climbing the Alps in the winter?"

Erin grinned. "I always wanted to try using an ice axe. It's trickier than it looks."

"The most adventurous I get is a hike in the local mountains," Diega said.

Erin stared out the window. "Maybe I'll see you up there sometime. You never know where you'll end up." She turned to Diega. "I'd better go find my mom."

The warning bell rang, summoning the students to line up in their designated areas outside. Diega grabbed her sunglasses and headed for the door. Erin accompanied her as far as the intersection of the hallways. Erin paused as if to say something, but then merely waved her hand before heading the opposite way toward the front office.

As Diega turned to head to the door to the playground, she saw a slender, older man rhythmically swishing a dust mop down the hall. He wore a blue custodian's uniform.

"Hola, Luis!" Diega called.

"Como esta, senorita?" Luis called in return.

As Luis looked at her, Diega noticed that his black hair was greying as was his mustache. "How's your daughter doing in college?"

A smile bloomed on Luis's face. "Juanita is graduating in June. With honors." He beamed even more. "So what can I do for you, Senorita Diega?"

"Did you clean my classroom after the police were finished with it?"

"Are there problems? Did I miss something? There was black powder everywhere and I tried to clean it all. There was even some under the counter."

After assuring Luis of the excellence of his work Diega asked, "Did you notice anything on the floor near the back counter? Something sticky?"

"Si. The police told me I had to be careful of that. You know the district has training on biohazards?" Luis thumped his chest. "I am one of the few who know how to properly dispose of this."

"Biohazard? What was that stuff?"

"Blood."

MORE CHAOS THAN usual greeted Diega when she reached the playground. Instead of students in separate lines, several mobs were darting around the yard chasing a small, black Labrador. Some of the teachers were trying to herd the students back; others were trying to capture the dog.

Diega noticed the only teacher not doing much of anything was Megan Beaker. As a mentor teacher, Diega was assigned a variety of new teachers to assist during their first two years on the job. This was Diega's second year with Megan, and she doubted that she had had any positive influence on the young woman.

The Lab ran up to Megan and sat down, tongue lolling from the side of its mouth. Megan jumped back and bent her knee as if to give the dog a kick.

"Grab her collar," Diega commanded, walking quickly to Megan's side.

Megan put her foot down and her hands up in front of her mouth. Diega leaned over and grabbed the dog's leather collar.

Diega eyed her mentee. "Were you really going to kick this poor, little guy?"

Megan opened her eyes wide and slowly back away. Her voice was muffled from behind her hands. "He scared me."

Diega shook her head as she dragged the Lab over to Luis who had followed her outside. How anyone could be afraid of a playful, friendly puppy, she could not imagine. She did not think it was possible, but Megan had dropped even further in her estimation. Why she had ever agreed to be a mentor was beyond Diega's recollection at that moment.

Dog delivered, Diega walked back to her class's area of the playground. Now that the excitement had ended, students were returning to their assigned spaces.

Diega saw her former classroom neighbor, Rita Morgan, standing with her hands clasped behind her body, waiting for the stragglers in her class to line up. Since Diega's class assembled next to Rita's on the playground, Diega detoured over to Rita's line.

"How are you doing?"

Rita looked down. "Not so great." She glanced up at Diega. "Nightmares."

Diega nodded. "I've had a few myself. Have the police been leaving you alone?"

Rita stepped away from her line. "Heavens, no. I guess they've been asking me the same questions they ask you. 'Who did you see?' 'What did you see?' 'What did you hear?'"

"Did you have any answers for them?"

Rita shrugged. "Not many. I got here around 7:15 and I noticed Zeke's car parked along the side of the building. I only remember because a pickup truck was pulling away from the curb and barely missed hitting his bumper. I thought I might be called as an accident witness..." She stopped and bit her lip, ruining the layer of deep red lipstick. "Then I realized I had left the spelling test at home. I've been so forgetful lately." She shook her head. "Anyway, I drove home, grabbed the test, and came back around 7:45 to find..."

The second bell rang signaling the beginning of the school day. Diega touched Rita lightly on the shoulder and said, "Take care. I've been thinking about you." As she said it, Diega realized it was true.

Rita looked as shocked as Diega felt for saying it. Her mouth opened and closed then she nodded and waved to her class.

Diega ambled over to her own students who were more or less in a line. She cleared her throat and the line straightened. She led them inside.

Sally Nelson was waiting for her at the door to her classroom. She glanced pointedly at her watch and then stared at Diega.

Diega turned to her class who were lined up in the hallway. "Go ahead in and put your things away. Joey, start the Pledge of Allegiance, and Anahit, please do the roll call. The reading assignments are on the board."

While her class filed in, Diega asked Sally what she wanted.

"Not me. Detective Theophilus. I've been sent by him to supervise your class. I presume you have lesson plans on your desk."

Bite me, Diega thought. "Under the blizzard of school memos. But I'm sure you can wing it if you have to." Diega sauntered down the hall in what she hoped was a nonchalant manner.

Detective Theophilus had once again commandeered the principal's office. He was shifting some papers around on Sally's desk. Diega stood in the doorway to the office until he lifted his head to acknowledge her. He picked up Sally's silver letter opener and leaned back in her leather chair. He twirled the sharp-edged instrument between his hands as he spoke.

"Every time I think I'm done with you, your name pops up again. It's beginning to make me a little curious." Theophilus laid down the letter opener and waved her to a seat. "Why did you go to Mr. Chambers's residence?"

"You mean yesterday?"

"Have there been other times?"

"No."

The detective only stared, a bland look on his face.

"Since I doubt I'll be going to the funeral, we took a plant to Mrs. Chambers."

The policeman nodded and wrote something. "Who's 'we'?"

"A good friend of mine offered to go with me." Diega did not think Tully would mind the characterization.

"And the name of this good friend?"

Diega supplied Tully's name and address and assured the detective that Tully had no acquaintance with the deceased or his family. Presuming the interview at an end, Diega stood and walked toward the door.

Theophilus raised a finger. "I only want to make sure of one thing. You were never at Zeke Chambers's house before Sunday? Not at a Christmas party? Not some afternoons perhaps? Maybe to drop something off for school or something? Maybe to discuss some other negotiation items?"

Diega turned and gripped the back of her chair. She leaned in the direction of the detective and said very slowly, "I have never been at that house before."

Again he nodded, looking down at his papers. "That's really interesting." He looked up and stared straight into Diega's eyes. "I just read a report from one of the other detectives. It seems Mr. Chambers's son swears he saw you at the house on several occasions."

Chapter Seven

THE VIBRATIONS FROM the music thumped Diega's chest before she could even hear the tune. Go Bar was the latest women's space to open in the San Fernando Valley and it was typical of the genre. Body-rattling music, small dance floor, a pool table, a few tiny booths along the walls, and a long horseshoe-shaped bar with a tattooed, tank-top wearing, curvaceous bartender behind it. Atypically, the lighting, although muted, was adequate, and the walls held paintings and photographs rather than posters and liquor signs.

Diega had decided that after her days of murder and mayhem, a burger, a beer, and a little community time were what she needed on a Friday night. She sipped her Pacifico while waiting for her mushroom and Swiss cheeseburger and scanned the sparsely populated room. Too early on a weekend for most partiers, it seemed to be only the regulars who propped themselves on the barstools and shouted encouragement to the ones poking the cue ball on the pool tables.

Light from the opening door announced a new arrival and Diega noticed that several of the barstool occupants took time to view a reddish-blond woman striding through the doorway.

Diega recognized her instantly. She watched as her principal's daughter marched to an isolated barstool and ordered. Diega could not see what the bartender was pouring, but it only involved one liquor bottle, no mixer, and very little ice. Erin Nelson raised the glass and stared at it for a moment before downing it in one long swallow. She pointed at the glass to order another.

One of the pool players cackled as she banked the eight ball into a side pocket. The woman was plump with short, spiky grey hair. As her opponent gathered the balls to re-rack them, Diega watched her scan the room. Eventually, she swung around to face Diega. She gave a slight nod, did a double take, and headed straight for Diega's table.

"Diega DelValle, as I live and breathe! Didn't know you were a bar kind of girl." She plunked herself on a chair beside Diega.

It was Diega's turn to do a double take. "Kathy, is that you? What did you do with your hair?"

Kathy Henshaw cackled again as she ran her hands over the buzz-cut sides of her hair. "Once I retired from that hell-hole you call GUSD, I decided to let my hair go natural and get a do I wanted to have all these years." She turned her head from side to side so that Diega could get the full effect. "Rather avant garde for Vista Elementary, don't you think? I've been thinking of adding purple stripes."

Kathy had been the school secretary for more years than anybody could remember, and Kathy was not about to enlighten them when anybody asked. She had retired last October. Diega was amazed at what four months wrought.

"Seems I got out of that place just in time. What the hell's going on at Vista anyway?" Kathy nodded at two newcomers who headed for the pool table. She waved her pool partner to another opponent and she and Diega compared notes. She was most curious about how Sally Nelson was doing since she had only been on the job three months when Kathy retired. "That woman is a control freak. Has her mind set on the superintendent's job. Probably explains the odd company she kept."

Diega raised an eyebrow, which was all the incentive Kathy needed.

"That creep Zeke Chambers from the district office—being dead doesn't make him any saint. He'd drop by all the time. In fact, some mornings I'd come in and she and Zeke were already in her office." Kathy shook her head. "You know Zeke had the super's ear. I bet Sally was greasing the tracks to the district office. Silly her. Zeke's been working for over a year to worm his ass into the super's chair."

The pool game ended, and with it a demand for Kathy's entry into the next round of play. The women each scribbled their phone numbers on paper napkins and exchanged them. "Keep in touch," Kathy said as she grabbed her pool cue.

Erin was still soaking up the booze when Diega's burger arrived. As Diega ate, she watched the principal's daughter consume three more servings of liquor and no food—not even the spicy mix of nuts and crackers on the bar.

Finished with her dinner, Diega left a tip on the table, grabbed her beer, and walked over to Erin's area of the bar. Diega leaned on the stool next to Erin.

Erin did not look up. "Not interested," she said, more to the glass in her hand than to Diega.

"I don't know about that. You seem very interested in that drink."

Erin looked this time and recognition filtered into her cool, blue eyes. She swung the glass somewhat in Diega's direction as if giving divine permission for one to enter her kingdom.

Diega sat. Up close she could see that Erin was even younger than her first estimate. The smooth checks and lack of smile lines dropped her age to mid- or late-twenties. Diega examined her and decided that even an unblemished face could not hold the anger Erin radiated without temporary furrows marring a forehead. Erin smacked the glass on the counter and asked for another.

Before the bartender could fill the order, Diega raised a warning finger at the tattooed woman. "Remember, you're liable if she leaves here and gets in an accident."

Erin rocked back on her stool and glared at Diega. She turned back to talk to the bartender, but that brilliant worker had suddenly found herself totally occupied at the other end of the bar.

"There are other bars in this world," Erin announced as she tried to pull some bills from the pockets of her Dockers. She ended up sliding into Diega, who propped her up and then helped her stand.

Diega sighed. "I think I'd better drive you home."

Erin grabbed the edge of the bar as she shook her head. "I don't have sex with strangers."

"Good policy," Diega said as she guided her out the door. "Where do you live?"

Erin waved her finger slowly back and forth. "Not there. My parents live there. Can't have them see me like this."

Diega sighed more deeply. She helped Erin into the passenger's seat of her trusty purple Hyundai and drove back to her own house.

The moment Diega got her front door open, Erin asked directions to the bathroom and dashed down the hall. The retching sounds were not a surprise to Diega.

Twenty minutes later, white-faced, woozy, but somewhat more sober, Erin perched herself on the edge of Diega's couch. "Your cats," she said, as she ran a cold washcloth over her face, "were of great assistance to me in there."

Diega grinned and handed Erin a tall glass of water. She knew BB and Sherwood thought they owned the bathroom. They somehow knew they had a captive audience and always presented themselves for petting. "They love to watch the water go down the drain. I can only imagine they were overjoyed to have someone down on the floor with them."

Diega dropped into the armchair opposite the couch. "Do you try to commit slow suicide often?"

"Believe me, when suicide becomes my choice, it will be fast." Erin leaned back and laid the cloth across her head.

Diega got no more from Erin that night. Between fits of nausea, Erin settled into the guest room. Diega offered to call Erin's parents and tell them where she was, but Erin brushed it aside. Diega was relieved since she could not quite picture calling her boss and explaining this particular situation.

Saturday morning was crisp and clear. Diega wrapped herself in her long chenille robe and sat out on the back deck with a pot of hot, black coffee, the morning paper and two cats determined to inspect their domain.

Half an hour later, Diega heard scuffling from inside the house. Erin appeared, still in the sweatpants and heavy T-shirt that Diega had loaned her to sleep in. Her wavy hair was plastered to the left side of her head as if she had hit the bed and not moved all night. She groaned as she sat in the chair next to Diega. Wordlessly, Diega poured a cup and handed it to her. Erin gave a weak smile of thanks and took several swallows of the coffee before speaking.

"I feel like a teeny tiny tanker truck exploded in my head."

Diega made a noncommittal noise.

"I hope..." Erin began, then looked at Diega and shrugged.

Diega thought of her own not-always-wisely-spent youth and bit back a comment.

Erin swept her arm out indicating the lawn and gardens of Diega's backyard. "You've done a lot of work here."

"I started in on it a couple of years ago. It's a good way to work off aggravation."

"Your students or my mother?"

Diega raised both eyebrows.

Erin grinned. "I asked her about you and I got a short lecture on rebellious know-it-alls who, just because they're good, think they don't have to follow the rules." She refilled her cup. "Sound like anyone you know?"

Diega grabbed the pot from Erin and filled her own cup. "If you want to clean up before breakfast, I put out some towels and a washcloth in the guest bath. There's shampoo and conditioner in the shower. Do you want a change of clothes? I might have something that would fit you."

"I see the subject has officially been changed. I'll take you up on the shower and clothes. Breakfast is a maybe. Let's see if my stomach is still speaking to me."

"YOU HAVE A nice collection of CDs and records," Erin said as she perused Diega's living room bookshelf after breakfast. She had surprised Diega by not only consuming her portion of an omelet but also several pieces of sourdough toast. Now she wandered the living room while waiting for a cab she had insisted upon calling so that she could get back to the bar and retrieve her car. "Jazz, classic rock, and show tunes. Quite eclectic."

"What kind of music do you like?"

Erin shrugged. "Hip-hop, country, and classical mainly."

"Talk about eclectic. Classical?"

Another shrug. "I took piano lessons from the time I was six. I liked it and I grew to love the music."

"Do you still play?"

Erin shook her head. "I have some numbness in my fingers. I'm hoping it will go away, but until then I make do with listening."

Diega sensed there was more to the tale, but did not push. "And where does country fit in?"

"The story. Hip-hop is for moving, dancing, cleaning the house. Classical is for relaxing, thinking, and dreaming. Country is when I want a good cry." She laughed, as if to dispel the notion of ever needing to cry. The smile was dimmer but still in evidence as she looked straight at Diega. "I want to thank you for your extraordinary hospitality to someone you picked up at a bar."

Diega gave a little bow then raised a finger. "A bit of advice: don't always rely on the kindness of strangers."

Erin laughed again as she picked up a paper bag containing her clothes from the night before. The smile faded as she faced Diega. "Thank you for making me laugh. That's in short supply right now." She squeezed Diega's upper arm. "Stay well, my knight in shining armor."

Diega watched as the cab drove Erin away. She wondered why a woman who so obviously enjoyed life would be in misery. Was it merely a coincidence that her return, the murder, and her depression all happened simultaneously? Diega's cynical side won. The only answer that made sense to her was no.

Chapter Eight

"NO, MOM, I'M not bringing a friend along with me this afternoon." Diega snorted into the receiver and decided that there were worse things than having her mother eager to meet whatever new woman might be in her life. Like the seven months when neither her mother nor father would speak to her after she had come out to them when she was twenty-four.

Given the fact that two of her closest friends had been disowned by their parents and one woman she knew in South Carolina was fighting being fired from her teaching job because of being gay, the gentle nudges Diega got from her mother about settling down were a wonderful problem to have. Lately the nudges included talk of couples her mother had heard about that were having and raising children together.

Diega was amazed that her mother was even interested in another grandchild. She was personally convinced that the seven grandchildren Diega's five other siblings had given her should be enough for any woman. Obviously her mother disagreed. "Do you bug Anita about bringing a guy to lunch?"

"Your sister is as stubborn as you are. I offered to invite Ramona's son this afternoon so she could meet him, but she said no. My two unmarried children. I worry."

Diega considered skipping the family's traditional Saturday midday meal. Then again, maybe she and her baby sister, Anita, could link arms against her mother's onslaught. She checked on one last deciding factor, the presence or absence of her homophobic, religious zealot of an older sister, Lupe. "Is our other sis coming?"

"No. She has a church meeting."

Silently thanking the universe for keeping Lupe busy with something other than disapproving of her way of life, Diega asked what she could bring to lunch besides a date.

Diega arrived at the family home in Pasadena that afternoon armed with her contribution of two loaves of sourdough bread, which were swept away from her and replaced with an armful of her mother's ample body.

Diega felt it was too much to be hoped that news of the murder at her school had escaped her family's notice. She was right.

"So when were you going to tell me about this maniac who's running up and down the halls of your school killing people?" Diega's mother, Helena, pushed Diega away from her. She shook her head at her daughter, her still naturally reddish-brown hair vibrating with the movement.

"Mom, this isn't Paducah, Kentucky. There was no mentally ill teen with a gun. Only one person was killed and he doesn't even work at Vista."

"So tell me you're not involved with this." She fixed her deep brown eyes onto Diega's. "Not that you'd tell me the truth anyway. Like last time when your mother had to read about you in the papers."

Before Diega could respond to the same complaint she had heard for the last few years, she felt strong arms encircle her and she was lifted off her feet and spun around. She knew precisely who was attacking her, for Uncle Juan had greeted her this way for as long as she could remember. She thought when she reached her teens or twenties or thirties that he would stop. Now Diega realized happily that Uncle Juan would probably pick her up and spin her even if he had to do it from a wheelchair.

"Put me down, you brute!" Diega thumped playfully on his slim, hairy arms.

"Mi hija," Uncle Juan said, as her released her. "You have been the talk of the gathering once again."

"I can only imagine." Diega slid her arm through his and together they entered the fray.

The topic of conversation was, indeed, the murder at Diega's school. Diega's two older brothers and their spouses, her sister, Anita, and her father were all agog to hear her account. Since five of Diega's nephews and nieces were also wandering through the living room, she tried to keep the details G-rated.

Her fifteen-year-old nephew, Frank, was not cooperating. "So you actually saw him lying there dead? Were there maggots or flies? Detectives can tell a lot about the time of death by the insects found in the wounds."

Frank's mother, Stephanie, whacked him on his head. "No more Patricia Cornwell novels for you." Stephanie was Diega's favorite sister-in-law. Only two years senior to Diega, they had bonded over politics, music, movies, and books. Diega thought her brother, Hernando, had exhibited superb taste in marrying her.

Uncle Juan cleared his throat and steered the topic away from the gore. "I actually knew the fellow, too."

Diega was not the only family member to gape at Juan.

He shrugged. "Not like our little Diega knew him, maybe, but I recognized his picture in the *Times*. I've seen him around the Triple Aces Club."

Uncle Juan was a professional gambler and was well-known on the poker circuit. Diega knew that when Juan was in town he played Texas Hold 'Em at the card clubs in both Gardena and the city of Commerce. He was one of the high-stakes players and would even occasionally sit in on the no-limit games. Diega mentally compared the amount of money needed to play in those games with the amount of Zeke's salary.

The gap made the Grand Canyon look like a crack in the sidewalk.

Diega raised an eyebrow at Juan. "Did Zeke actually play at the high-stakes tables?"

"I never saw him at the no-limit games, but I saw him a lot at the ten-twenty table."

Although gambling for Diega extended only as far as poking the buttons on a penny slot machine, she knew her uncle was referring to a game where players put in an ante of ten dollars and could raise twenty dollars a shot.

"Was he any good?" Diega asked.

Juan shrugged. "I never really played with him. He must have done okay. He kept coming back for more."

Diega's father laughed. "Oh sure. Only winners keep coming back. Right, Juan?"

"My dear brother, haven't you ever talked with poker players? They all win, every time. Ask them."

Diego DelValle patted his younger brother on the cheek on his way into the kitchen to help serve dinner. He looked over his broad shoulder at his daughter. "The only thing you can count on with gamblers is that they lie, each and every one of them."

BACK HOME AFTER her family gathering, Diega felt restless. She decided that too much sitting, talking, eating, and lazing about led to thinking, brooding, and gaining weight, three activities she wanted to avoid. The alternative was exercise, so she changed into shorts and a T-shirt and jogged down a few streets to the Chandler bike path that Burbank had constructed over what had once been railroad tracks. Since nearly losing her life crossing Clark Street, Diega had changed jogging routes and, for the last several months, had joined the other ten percent of her fellow Burbank citizens who derived, if not pleasure, then at least satisfaction from a brisk walk or run down the new bike corridor that led into North Hollywood.

Diega padded lightly down the path, which was lined with trees and dark green lantana. Her jog had reached the tempo where the pumping of her legs and arms felt effortless. She enjoyed those moments since she knew this would soon be followed by the push to exceed her comfort zone. Once a week she went farther and faster than the previous week. This was her day.

As Diega started to pick up speed, she looked ahead and saw a flashing light reflecting off two iridescent strips attached to the outside of a pair of fluorescent green running shorts. Without even being able to clearly see the person's face, Diega knew it was either a lost Martian or Jack O'Reilly approaching her. She stopped and hailed the figure. "No pups today?"

Jack wiped sweat from his freckled forehead with his wristband

and moved into the shade of a nearby tree. "The little angels are having a bit of a lie-in today. I took them to Santa Monica yesterday and what with their frolicking in and out of the water and up and down the beach, the little beasties wore themselves out."

Diega smiled at the Irish lilt that colored Jack's speech. Ever since he had acted as a guardian angel when Diega was attacked while jogging, the two had taken to stopping to chat when their exercise outings coincided.

"I haven't seen you lately," Diega said.

"I'm looking to run in a 10K, so I've started expanding my horizons, don't you know. In fact, I've taken to running through the park by your school. You're at Vista Elementary, aren't you? Maybe I'll drop by and see you sometime."

"Come during school time and bring the girls. I'm sure my students would be delighted to meet dogs that are almost as tall as they are."

"It's a date." Jack readjusted his blinking reflectors. The lights bounced off his neon green shorts providing his thin torso with a glowing aura. Finally satisfied with his adjustments, he looked up and said, "I read about the murder there. You are staying safe now, are you not, lassie? Not going to undo any of my good work?"

Since coming to her rescue a couple of years back, Jack frequently exhibited overprotective tendencies. Diega clapped him on the back. "If I ever feel I need some protection I'll borrow your two brutes." His German Shepherds, Maggie and Abby, were siblings whose mother could have been mistaken for a small horse.

"Aye, and you're counting on my girls to pounce on the culprit and lick him to death, I suppose." With a snort and a shake of his head, Jack bounded down the cement pathway.

Diega smiled to herself as she once again picked up speed. The faster her feet pounded on the pavement, the more her mind opened and free-flowing thoughts drifted in and out of her consciousness. Only slowly did she become aware that some of those thoughts were sticking around and trying to make themselves heard.

One of the most persistently niggling questions involved Erin. What would make a young, energetic, and definitely attractive woman drink herself into a stupor?

The ring of the telephone greeted Diega as she entered the back door of her house, sweaty from her jog. She lunged for the instrument, tripping over her cats on the way.

"My favorite niece!"

"Uncle Juan. What a pleasure to hear your smiling voice, especially after seeing you only a few hours ago." Diega tucked the phone between her shoulder and ear as she tended to the ritual of feeding her cats their dinner.

"I was wondering if you'd like to join me at the Triple Aces Club tonight."

"Me? At a poker club? The last of the big-time gamblers? The one who can't remember if a straight beats a flush?"

"That's the person I had in mind. Too bad it would be unethical to play at the same table with you. I might make enough in one evening to retire permanently."

"Not with my penny-ante bets." Diega placed the cats' dishes on the floor. BB sniffed at her bowl, scratched at the floor as if she could cover the food with the vinyl, and walked away, tail held high. Sherwood had no such reservations. After quickly inhaling her mashed meat, she proceeded to consume BB's portion as well. Diega shook her head. "Is it 'Bring a Clueless Relative to the Club' night?"

Juan laughed. "No, but I'll suggest that. We always need fresh suckers. It's hard to bluff the same people over and over." He explained that some of the people who had played with Zeke would probably be at the club on a Saturday evening. "I thought maybe you'd like to talk with them."

"Why would I want to do that?"

Her uncle sounded a bit sheepish. "I know you've done this investigating thing before and I thought I could help you out this time."

Diega moaned. "Uncle Juan, I was kind of forced into looking into that particular murder." Mostly, she corrected herself mentally, but did not amend her statement out loud. "I really think the police should be given the chance to solve this one on their own."

"Oh."

Her uncle sounded so disappointed that Diega almost relented.

Juan tried again. "The prime rib dinner is only five dollars for players."

"Oh, yeah. Mom's feast wasn't quite enough for one day."

"I'm buying."

Diega thought of Theophilus's contention that Zeke had a handful of her hair clasped in his cold, dead hand. She thought of Zeke's help with negotiations. She thought of his bloodied hand, outstretched as if asking for help. She suspected she would regret it, but somehow she could not stop herself. "Sold."

Chapter Nine

THE EXTERIOR NEON lights announcing the Triple Aces Club bounced across the clouds in the evening sky. Diega had agreed to meet her uncle at the casino at seven. Juan would have preferred meeting at nine with dinner at eleven. Diega conceded that some people might be forgiven for confusing her uncle with a vampire since he rarely left the house when the sun was out.

Diega entered the sliding glass doors and stood on the deck overlooking the pit where the first-floor poker games were played. The noise of a hundred subdued conversations filled the air. Unlike Vegas or other gambling meccas, no noisy slot machines clanged nor did neon lights flash. In this city, the only gambling allowed were games of "skill," not chance. Diega had never understood what skill had to do with what cards you were dealt, but such was the law. The one thing that this club had in common with the Vegas casinos was an absence of clocks. Gambling places did not seem to wish to remind their customers of the number of hours they were whiling away. Diega had to check her wristwatch to see if she was, as usual, running early.

"Diega? Diega DelValle?"

Diega turned toward the voice. The short man facing her was vaguely familiar. He wore a white golf shirt that stretched over his rounded belly. His sandy-red hair was gelled straight back. For a moment Diega could not figure out if he was a parent or a fellow teacher. She was grateful that he did not call her "Ms. DelValle" because that would have identified him as a former student. She had been feeling old enough without that to add insult to her injured ego. Finally her memory synapse turned up a name. "Harrison?"

Harrison Carter fell into the fellow Glendale school district teacher category, although he taught middle school. He and Diega had met as part of a training program to help improve science teaching across all levels of the district. Diega had not seen him for at least two years, yet here he was greeting her like she was his best buddy.

He grinned with gusto. "I've heard you're a wild woman, but I didn't think that included gambling."

"You're right. My wildness is limited. I'm actually meeting someone for dinner."

Harrison nodded. "Wise move. Save your money." He looked around as if assessing his surroundings. "Of course," he said, over his shoulder and somewhat directed at Diega, "if you wanted to feel like part of the action, but you don't want to be the one at the table, I might be able to help you out."

Diega stuffed her hands into the pockets of her slacks and waited.

At her silence, Harrison swung around to once again face her. "If you wanted to invest a couple of hundred in a poker game, I would be willing to play it for you and we could split the winnings." He raised his eyebrow at Diega, inviting her to comment on his magnanimous offer.

Diega rejected the first three responses that came to mind as being, in order, too uncouth, too profane, and too degrading. She finally smiled and said, "P.T. Barnum's sucker is somewhere else at this minute."

Harrison flushed causing freckles to pop out on his cheeks. "I was trying to cut you in on a good deal. My luck is turning. I can feel it. With a little cash I could..."

"End up even more in debt." Juan DelValle said as he slid his arm around his niece's shoulder. "Please excuse me while I escort this exquisite creature to a culinary experience unlike anything outside of McDonald's."

Leaving a dejected Harrison Carter behind, Diega asked, "Do you know him?"

Juan shook his head. "I know a hundred like him. If he's smarter than most, he'll steer clear of the professional money lenders."

"Loan sharks?"

Juan nodded. "Not nice people. And not a nice topic for such a wonderful evening. Let me introduce you to my world."

Juan escorted Diega along the plush, wildly colored carpeted ramp of blue, green, and gold that led to the playing floor. He toured her through the lower level poker games and the specialty games such as Pai Gow. He then led her upstairs to the soundproofed high-stakes room where several players greeted Juan with handshakes while others scowled.

Leading Diega by the elbow, Juan took her over to a side room with three tables in it. "This is where they teach people to play the different games. Do you want to start here while I scout around and see who I can turn up?"

Relieved not to have to part with any money yet, Diega took a seat at the Texas Hold 'Em tutoring table. The dealer had started to explain the three-card flop that was the second step in the game, so Diega knew she had not missed much. The lesson took her over much of what she had gleaned from her uncle's many stories. She felt confident until the dealer started in on the betting rules. Somewhere during the discussion of the big blind, the little blind, the antes, the betting limits, and which hands beat which, it became even more evident to Diega that she did not have the gambling gene.

Still, she stayed on and played five hands with the other neophytes, losing four before lucking into a pocket pair of kings that resulted in a full house. Thanking them all for the experience, she escaped in search of her uncle.

Diega people-watched as she wandered through the lower level of the casino. She spotted a young man in jeans and a brown motorcycle jacket in earnest conversation with an older man who was dressed all in black. She hesitated when she recognized the youngster as Wayne Chambers, Zeke's motorcycle-riding son, then deliberately detoured around behind the men. She edged to within eavesdropping distance. She positioned her back to Wayne in case he turned around, but she was able to watch the older man out of the side of her eye.

"No way, kid," the man in black was saying. "You don't know what you're talking about."

"You know I can get it," Wayne said, nervously stroking his budding mustache. "I only want the same deal my dad had."

"Kid, I don't know what kind of deal you've got in mind, but I'm not interested. Now get the hell out of here before the floor men start nosing around. They don't like children anywhere near the playing floor."

The way the man said it, Diega guessed there was a contemptuous look on his face. She became sure of it when Wayne exploded.

"Look, punk, I'm twice the man my father was, and even he was a better man than a gangbanger like you. So you watch who you're dissing."

Diega watched as two bulky men, who had obviously indulged in steroids sometime in their recent past, started toward Wayne and his antagonist. The man in black waved them off with a flick of his hand, his eyes never leaving Wayne's face.

His voice became quieter and lower. "Get your finger out of my face or lose it and half the arm it's attached to."

The cold tone made Diega want to cringe. It must have had the same effect on Wayne because he pushed past her and headed straight for the exit.

When Diega turned, the man in black was adjusting his suit jacket all the while staring at Wayne's fleeing back.

If looks could kill, Zeke would soon have company in the family plot.

"There you are."

Diega jumped at the sound off her uncle's voice. "Sorry. I was looking for you and then got engrossed by the people. Guess I fell asleep on my feet."

"Then you need sustenance. We'll forego the player's discount and live it up by paying full price for the prime rib." Juan wrapped his arm around Diega's waist and leaned close to her ear. "It's a better place to talk. And I've got some things to tell you."

The restaurant was next to a hair salon on the upper deck of the casino.

Diega said, "All you need is a rent-a-cot business and no one would ever need to leave."

Juan hooked his thumb over his shoulder. "They've got a four-star hotel attached to this casino. If the owners had their way they'd build condos."

They slid into a corner booth far away from the other dozen occupants of the restaurant. The booth was beside the railing and overlooked the floor above the playing pit. After the waitress took their orders, Juan started his report.

"I talked to three regulars who played with your Zeke guy. One said Zeke liked to bet big and bluff often. One pegged him as liking to chase flushes. None of them thought much of him as a player. But they seemed to think he was not one to throw bad money after good."

"What kind of game did he play?"

"Hold 'Em. Mostly the ten- to twenty-dollar level."

Diega did some fast mental math. "Those pots could be in the $100 to $600 range."

"Or more. Depends on the flop and the players. It'd be easy to drop a thousand in a night if you were on the losing end of things."

"How often did Zeke come here?"

"According to my sources, he used to come three to four times a week. It'd been less lately."

"Lately? Like in the last how long?"

"They weren't sure, but it had been at least a month. He started coming in only for a few hours once or twice a week. They thought it might have something to do with his girlfriend."

"Girlfriend? You sure it wasn't his wife?" Diega accepted her salad from the waitress. She stabbed a piece of romaine and chewed thoughtfully.

Juan wiped his mouth with a cloth napkin. "That's the term they used. I wasn't sure whether or not he was married, so I didn't push the issue. Two of the guys mentioned a woman in her late thirties, early forties who was quite a looker. Maybe that was his wife. But Gerry said he'd seen a younger brunette hanging around recently. Of course, Gerry's seventy years old, so who knows what 'younger' might mean to him." Juan suddenly jumped up and waved his hand. A small, slim, Asian woman soon joined them in the booth.

"Hun Wong," the woman said, shaking hands with Diega. "But you can call me Honey."

"That's one of the names we call her," Juan said with a grin. "It's not the one we choose when she's beating the pants off us. Honey's one of the best pro gamblers on the circuit." He motioned the waitress over and ordered a coffee for Honey. "I was telling my niece here about that fellow who was killed last Friday. You know, the one who used to play here all the time."

"Slick boy Zeke. I knew him." Honey added two packets of sugar substitute and some non-dairy cream to her coffee. After tasting it she said, "Good looking guy. Very sexy. But he had the card sense of a two-year-old. Still, he seemed to get lucky a lot."

Diega asked, "Did you ever see him with a woman?"

Honey laughed. "The better question was did I ever see him without one. That man had more women hanging over him than ants on a picnic basket. The ones I felt sorry for were the ones who didn't play. They mostly sat on the balcony and read magazines waiting for him to get his fill for the evening."

"Was he with anybody in particular lately?"

Honey pursed her reddened lips. "Last time I saw him he was heading out the door with some sweet young thing. Her hair was in a French braid and she was thinner than his usual fare. Never saw her face. That was maybe a week or so before he was killed."

The sound of glass breaking made them all look over the railing to the deck above the playing pit.

The remnants of a lamp lay on its side. Beside it, two men were squared off against each other. Even as security police swarmed to them, the one Diega had immediately recognized as her fellow teacher, Harrison Carter, took a swing at the other man who was dressed all in black—the man who had earlier been arguing with Zeke's son. That man easily avoided the obviously drunken swing and Harrison toppled over onto a table.

The pit bosses and the security forces arrived simultaneously. They hauled Harrison to his feet. Their presence, however, did not seem to blunt his anger.

Harrison cursed the other man's heritage and questioned his parent's marital status. He raged at the two security guards holding his arms. "You want a big time bust, grab him. That son of a bitch is a murderer."

Chapter Ten

THE PARTY THE next evening was in the community room and pool deck of Felicia's apartment building. Diega guessed that Jenny and Felicia must have invited everyone they had ever met along with a few people they saw on the street. The community room was packed and the poolside area, warmed by outdoor heating stands, looked like a Manhattan mob scene in a movie.

The birch trees that surrounded the patio area were softly lit with ground floodlights. Twinkling white lights wound their way through hedges that hid the chain link fencing that guarded the pool's grounds. Small tables were scattered around the poolside. They boasted glass globes with flickering candles held in place by multicolored stones. People occupied every square millimeter of the space that was not claimed by flowerbeds.

Diega slid her way around the chatty hoards in search of the food table. Felicia had pointed her in that direction, but Diega was beginning to believe that the table's existence was a fable. Just as she decided that starvation would strike, a clump of humanity moved aside and a twelve-foot table covered with gastronomic delights faced her.

Unfortunately, she was still not alone at the filling station. Among the people already at the table was the one person Diega had hoped not to encounter this evening.

Evie Taylor and Diega had been a couple when Diega's temporary bout of infidelity broke up their relationship. Over the next year, they had attempted a reconciliation, but Evie's basic trust in Diega had been broken and Diega had been unable to overcome her own commitment phobia. In the years since, Evie had become involved with Marsha, a criminal defense attorney, while Diega had become involved with her cats and her garden and occasional speed dating.

To Diega's surprise, she found she was unsure of her feelings about this meeting. Embarrassment, guilt, and the ache of failure all vied for center stage. Berating herself for her cowardly hesitation, Diega stepped forward and greeted her ex-lover. They shared a polite hug and all the pleasantries that near strangers exchange while waiting to board a plane.

Diega wished she really had a flight to catch so that she would have a reason for breaking away from a banal conversation with someone who had once been the most important person in her life.

Evie, however, was the one who broke through the chitchat. "I heard about the murder at your school."

Diega nodded, not sure she wanted to go down this memory lane with Evie either.

"I suppose it's too much to expect that you aren't a key witness."

Diega felt redness creeping up her neck.

Evie sighed and shook her head. Her eyes were tender behind the lenses of her round glasses. She reached out and brushed her long, slender fingers along Diega's cheek. "Please take care of yourself." With another shake of her head, she was gone.

Diega had no time to process her feelings. Gwen Gunther, a private school operator, bumped against Diega as she turned to fill her plate along the banquet line. Gwen was a robust woman with wavy black hair that she let fall down her back. Her beak-like nose was her most prominent feature, but her warm brown eyes were what most people noticed first.

"Diega!" Gwen said, as she re-balanced her piled-high plate and wine glass to give Diega a squeeze.

"Hey, Gwen! How do you know Felicia and Jenny?"

"My husband worked with Jenny at the hospital." She waved a hand at the crowd. "He's out there somewhere. I'll have to introduce you two." She grabbed a carrot and chomped on it.

Diega added mainly vegetables to her plate to atone for her overindulgences of the day before. "I hear your company is branching out. Jumping into this new charter schools arena. How's it going?"

"Thriving. We've put in for a federal grant. If we get it, watch out world!"

"It's amazing that someone has found a way to make money off of public education."

"You say that like it's a bad thing." Gwen waved the carrot stick in the air. "I'd rather know the vast majority of my tax dollars were going into the classroom rather than into a bureaucracy."

"There I agree with you. But what percentage is really going to directly benefit the kids?"

"In the usual district, about seventy percent is classroom costs. In ours, it's ninety."

Diega did a quick calculation. Even ten percent of a million dollars added up to a handsome chunk of change. She was awoken from her reverie by the mention of a familiar name.

"I heard about Zeke Chambers. Not much of a loss on the humanity front, but a shame anyway." Gwen's deep brown eyes grew larger. "Oh dear, that was rather thoughtless of me. He wasn't a close friend or anything, was he?"

No knowing how to answer that, Diega parried with a question of her own. "How did you know Zeke?"

"Business. You know how we've been contracted to create charter schools in some of the districts in the San Fernando Valley?" She stopped. A smile slowly bloomed across her face. "Speaking of which, I've got an opening for a lead instructor at the new school in Chatsworth. You'd set the tone for the school. You'd be in charge of your own curriculum. No politics. No unions. Just focus on the students and their learning. Plus bonuses for exceptional merit."

Diega was nonplused. "You're offering me a job?"

Gwen nodded. "I've been in your classroom, and I've seen you at your Board of Ed meetings. You're smart and dedicated and a leader. I think you'd be perfect."

The idea was startling enough to Diega that it momentarily took precedence over her focus on nourishment.

Gwen patted Diega's shoulder. "I can see I threw you a curve with that one. Let's say I'll give you a call next week. By then I'll have more details, and you'll have more questions. I might even have a job opportunity closer to home."

"You're opening a charter school in Burbank?"

"Not yet," Gwen said, "although we're thinking about that. I do have an offer I'm going to put before the Glendale Board of Ed."

"I haven't heard this on the usually reliable grapevine. How long has it been in the works?"

"I've been trying to work with your district for over six months."

"What's the hold up?"

"Hold up." Gwen laughed bitterly. "A perfect term. Someday we'll have to have a long chat about that as well."

An hour later Diega felt partied out. She had talked and drank and finally eaten. Her body was trying to tell her that a party lasting past ten would not be a good combination with her Monday morning rising time of 5:00 a.m.

Before Diega could depart, Jenny grabbed her by the arm. "I need to talk to you."

Jenny led Diega over to a private side yard. Felicia and Tully were already there. Tully and Diega exchanged a quizzical look.

Jenny slipped an arm around Felicia waist. "There was an ulterior motive for the party. This is kind of Felicia's goodbye to her apartment building."

Diega and Tully's twin questioning looks transferred to Felicia's face.

"My lease is up at the end of the month, so I'm moving in with Jenny."

Before Diega could react, Tully burst out, "Are you out of your ever-lovin' minds?"

Chapter Eleven

AFTER RECOVERING FROM her immediate reaction to the news, Tully had declared that if Jenny and Felicia were going to do such a damn foolish thing, the least she and Diega could do, would be to throw a party for them. Despite Felicia's and Jenny's fervent protests that a party was exactly what they were having right then, Tully would have none of it.

"Not the same," Tully had said, as she wrapped an arm around each of her friends. "This may be a moving-away party, not that you let anyone know. What we'll throw is a moving-in one."

Diega had not a clue as to what a moving-in-together Tully-style event might include, but she was sure it would be memorable.

Diega was still pondering what form all that might take Monday as she walked down the empty halls of Vista Elementary, footsteps clacking loudly in the early morning. She unlocked her classroom, dumped her purse, opened the blinds, and unhooked the transom windows above the doors.

Humming, she pulled out sheets with origami patterns printed on them. Diega happily anticipated one of her favorite lessons combining reading, art, and writing. She would assign each student a partner. One partner would read the directions to the other. The one following the directions would cut out and fold the origami shape. Then the partners would switch roles. Diega found it to be an excellent way to introduce the concept of a process essay.

Diega opened her top desk drawer and pulled out her teacher's shears. As she held them, the vision of Zeke's body with the same style of scissors protruding from his back exploded in her head. She laid them back down, slid the desk drawer closed, and shut her eyes. She concentrated on slowing her breathing. Once she calmed down, she decided she'd demonstrate the lesson using a pair of her student's scissors instead.

When she pulled out her rack of student scissors, Diega remembered having loaned Jim's class half of her supply. She checked the clock. It was only 7:15 and Jim would probably not arrive until 8:00. That would leave her no time to finish the setup.

Knowing her key would not open Jim's classroom, Diega went in search of the custodian.

Diega stuck her head into the hallway. It was empty and silent. "Luis?" she called. Hearing no response, she peeked down the primary grades' wing of the school. Room E was open. She walked down and popped her head into the classroom. "Hey, Cindy."

A natural redhead with freckles, Cindy had a pale complexion at the best of times. Now she blanched even whiter as she leapt at the sound of Diega's voice. Clutching her chest she said, "Don't you ever sneak up on me like that again, Diega. I thought you were some crazed killer come after me."

"A crazed killer would know your name?"

"He might. I bet he knew Zeke Chambers's name."

"Point taken. I didn't actually come down here to test your reflexes. I'm looking for Luis. Have you seen him?"

"Not this morning." Cindy frowned. "I usually see him when I come in. There aren't too many of us early birds, you know. You don't think something has happened to him, too, do you?"

"Paranoia does not become you. He's probably cleaning up some mess. You wouldn't have some student scissors I could borrow?"

Cindy grabbed a pair out of her desk. "Blunt ends?"

"Thanks, but my troops would be insulted. I'll find Luis."

Cindy slid her desk drawer shut. "Let me come with you. You've got me worried now."

The rooms around Cindy's class were all closed. They returned to Diega's hall where some signs of life were stirring, but none of the later arrivals had seen Luis either.

Cindy said, "Maybe he's sick today."

"Then there'd be a sub." Diega pointed to the end of the hall. "Let's see if there are any tools missing from the custodian's closet. It might tell us where he's working."

The door was unlocked. Diega pulled it open and flipped on the light. Luis lay sprawled, face down, over a jumble of buckets and mops. A silver knife protruded from his back.

"IF I LIVED in Glendale, I'd move," Tully said, sipping her iced tea as she sat on the love seat in Diega's living room. "Look what Jessica Fletcher did to the population of Cabot Cove."

"If you are trying to equate me with the hand of death, I really don't appreciate it right now." Diega was slumped on her couch. "Thank God Luis has a chance to pull through."

"You've said that about three thousand times in the last fifteen minutes." Tully lumbered over and grabbed a washcloth from the kitchen. She rinsed it under cold water, wrung it out, and placed it on Diega's forehead.

Diega wiped her face with the cloth. "I will say I've gotten my money's worth out of all the first aid courses I've taken."

"How's your stomach?"

"Better." Diega eased herself up. "I cannot believe that anyone would hurt Luis. He's such a great guy, a hard worker, a real family man."

"Since your police buddy Theo says nothing seemed to have been stolen, my hunch is this is tied to Zeke's murder. I'd wager your beloved custodian was probably a man who knew too much or saw too much." Tully threw her body into an armchair. "So what could he have seen or heard or know that would get him stabbed in the back and why didn't he tell it to the police?" She fingered the fabric of the chair. "Of course, he wouldn't tell the police if he were trying to do something stupid like blackmail the murderer."

Diega started to shake her head then thought of Luis's daughter at USC. Maybe he saw a way of decreasing her college debts? She found the thought hard to square with the Luis she knew, but then, how well do you really know the people you work with?

Tully broke into her thoughts. "Then again, maybe he didn't know he saw something. You know, when you're used to seeing or hearing something, you don't notice it when it happens. So maybe he saw someone or something that he sees every day, so he didn't tell the police 'cause he didn't think it was unusual."

"That would make sense, otherwise he would have spoken up on Friday. But if that's the case, I wonder if we'll ever know what triggered this." Thinking of witnesses, Diega added, "Did I tell you that Wayne Chambers says he's seen me at their house in Glendale several times?"

"No, good buddy. You left that choice tidbit out of your otherwise thorough reports." Tully crunched some ice. "It sure looks as if the motorcycle maniac is lying through his newly-sprouted mustache. The question is why?"

"I was hoping you might have some bright ideas."

"Ideas, always. As to their wattage..." Tully hummed for a few seconds. "As far as I can see we've got three possibilities. One, he's lying. Two he's delusional. Three, he made a mistake."

"He didn't seem the hallucinating type, although with kids and drugs nowadays, who can tell? As for lying, I hardly know the kid. What would he have against me that he'd want to make me into a suspect?" Diega got up and placed the washcloth on a rack to dry. "But if he isn't lying, then I'd love to know who it was that he mistook me for."

"Now why would you want to know who it was?"

"So I could tell Theophilus to go bother that person instead. I'm tired of my name popping up on his radar."

"Uh uh." Tully's noncommittal tone clearly communicated disbelief.

Diega waited, but no further comments ushered forth. "I'm not running off to investigate this myself, if that's what you meant."

"Sure. Well, while you're busy not investigating this, you might want to know that the news is reporting that there's going to be an audit of the funds your buddy Zeke was in charge of for the district."

Diega recalled Gwen Gunther's veiled comments about Zeke.

The telephone rang before Diega could share that thought with

Tully. When she answered, Rita Morgan's voice came across the line.

Diega had to kick her social graces into gear. "Rita. This is a surprise." Diega choked on the understatement.

"I'm just checking on you. I heard you found poor Luis. I know how upsetting it was for both of us with Zeke and all..."

Not wanting to get into a touchy-feely discussion Diega asked, "How's Luis?"

"The police are only saying that he made it through the operation, but he's on life support now." Rita paused. "That doesn't sound good to me, but they're still saying he could pull through."

"How about school? Did the police close us down again?"

"They made all the upper grades go into the auditorium in the morning, but they're going to let the first four classes back into their rooms after lunch. I don't know what Rooms Ten, Twelve, and Thirteen are going to do. I guess I'm lucky I already have a trailer."

Diega was relieved that her room would be available tomorrow even though the rest of the hallway would be a ghost town. She flinched at her choice of words even as she thought them. "Any news about who might have attacked Luis?"

"Nothing was taken, so the police don't seem to think it was a robbery, even though we have those hoodlum boys with their baggy pants hanging down to their knees wandering the streets in the mornings. I told the police they should be looking into that. If nothing else, they're truant."

Rita's rant reminded Diega of one of the reasons why she avoided this woman. She was trying to think of a way out of the phone call—sudden relapse? earthquake? solar eclipse? –when Rita said, "It was odd about the knife, though."

"What was odd?"

"Oh, didn't I tell you? It was that silver letter opener of Sally's."

Chapter Twelve

THE CAT FIGHT started at three a.m. Tuesday morning. Sherwood and BB leapt atop Diega, biting and thrashing each other as if the World Wrestling Federation championship were on the line. BB managed to break away and thundered down the hall with Sherwood inches behind. Diega was left to ponder why she ever thought life without pets was somehow incomplete.

She rolled to her right side, trying to recapture the cloudy image of her dream. She was on a boat with several of the teachers from school. Evie was there as well. For some reason, Evie leapt into a lifeboat and started rowing away from the ship. Diega called out to her to wait, but Evie kept rowing. Equally inexplicably, Diega's mentee, Megan, was in the boat as well. Megan leaned into Diega and said, "Forget her. You should never have affairs with people you work with. They only lead to trouble."

AS DIEGA HEADED out the back door, the telephone rang. She yanked her purse higher on her shoulder, shifted her paper pile onto the arm holding her book bag, and reached the phone seconds before the answering machine could pick up the call.

"I'd like to make up for my beyond boorish behavior of the weekend." Erin Nelson sounded clear and sober. "I was wondering if you'd like to take a short hike with me this afternoon after school. I found a great place in the Verdugo Mountains and I'll provide a picnic dinner."

Diega considered what sounded suspiciously like a date. "That's a very nice offer, but—"

"I want to thank you for saving what little dignity I had left Friday night. No strings, I promise. Believe me, I'm not in any shape for strings."

Diega surprised herself by agreeing to join her. They set a time and meeting place and she dashed to work.

As Diega entered Vista Elementary, she heard a voice calling her that gave her cause to wonder if her dream was an example of precognition.

"Diega!" said Megan Beaker with her usual enthusiasm. "I wanted to talk with you about your science project."

Diega suppressed a sigh and turned to face her least favorite mentee. Diega had noticed that most of the younger women were wearing their hair long and straight with the only variation being with or without bangs. Megan was a brunette "with." She was a fashionable size zero with a pixie nose and wide brown eyes. Her mouth was also wide and frequently open, earning her Diega's private nickname of Motor Mouth Megan.

"I wanted to know if your unit on genetics would work with my class."

The concept was not even close to the science curriculum for fourth graders, a fact Diega was about to remind Megan of when Megan suddenly switched topics.

"Did you see that policeman who was here yesterday? He's creeping all over asking questions. How weird is that? None of us had anything to do with it. No one would think that would they?" She blinked her round eyes at Diega.

Diega was uncertain whether Megan really expected an answer, but she gave one anyway. "Zeke worked for the district and was killed in our school. Luis is our custodian. I think the police may well believe that someone connected with the GUSD is responsible for one or both of the attacks."

Megan leaned toward Diega, wagging her finger. "That's only if the two are linked. Poor Luis might have been knifed by some homeless person who was sleeping in the hallway. You can never tell what those people will do. They're mentally disturbed, you know. Of course, I don't know how a tramp would get hold of Sally's letter opener. At least, the gossip around the teacher's room said that was what was sticking out of Luis's back. Could be they're wrong. You know how gossip is." Megan paused for less time than it took a normal person to breathe and then continued. "I wonder if the police talked to Zeke Chambers's family. I've heard he had trouble with his kids. Now there's a genetics project for you." She leaned even closer. "Look, I've seen you talking to that detective. Maybe you should tell him about Zeke's family."

Diega drew back and raised her eyebrows. "First of all, Megan, if you have reliable information, go talk to Theophilus yourself. Secondly, until they arrest someone, the Glendale PD may be popping up frequently. So give up on your fantasy of them disappearing anytime soon." She unlocked the door to her classroom and shut it as quickly as possible to prevent Megan from following her inside.

EXACTLY AT THREE-THIRTY, Erin was at the front door of Diega's house. She wore blue jeans, a green short-sleeved shirt, and well-worn hiking boots. Diega was glad she had her own pair of boots, although it had been several years since she had used them. The last time had been three years ago with a backpacking group on a hike up Mount San Jacinto outside of Palm Springs. The boots had been collecting dust in the back of her closet since then. Unearthing them, Diega wondered when it was, exactly, that she had become old.

"I'll drive," Erin said and led Diega to a white, generic-looking sedan. "Rental," Erin said. "Not my usual style, but until I decide where I'm going to settle, I don't want the commitment of a car."

Diega thought of the time in her life, not too long ago, when being the caretaker of cats had seemed too much of a commitment. She concluded that maybe she had not aged as much as matured.

The white, wispy clouds stretching across the Verdugo mountaintops gave an indication of fair weather for their outing. Diega had once hiked a six-mile loop from Burbank to Glendale via a trail across the foothills right after a rain. The trek had been exhausting, but the views of the valley had proved worth it.

Erin swung the car past a metal gate and up a narrow road that led to Wildwood Canyon Park. On this weekday, unlike most weekends, there were abundant parking places along the paved entryway to the park.

Conversation had been minimal on the ten-minute drive from Diega's house to the park and it did not pick up much as the women strapped on their backpacks and headed up a cement sidewalk before cutting across to a dirt trailhead.

Erin took the lead. "It's pretty steep for the first leg, but it levels out past that."

Diega watched in awe as Erin strode up the sixty-degree incline as if it were flat land. She shook her head and followed at a more sedate pace. When she trudged around the second bend, Erin was there waiting for her. True to her promise, the trail was now at an incline that someone other than mountain goats might be able to transverse.

The scent of sage and dust made Diega fantasize about the settlers who had packed their most precious possessions and bounced their way along the dirt roads and mountain passes to reach these hills. Diega paused and gazed at the brown scrub. She hoped they had not been too disappointed.

The crest of the hill not only offered a panoramic view of the San Fernando Valley but a picnic table and benches kindly provided by the city of Burbank. Diega was banished to a rock by the overlook while Erin laid out their early supper.

Erin called out, "I asked my mom if you were a vegetarian. She didn't seem to think so, so I took a chance on chicken. It free-range with no hormones."

Diega assured her that meat of almost any kind was fine with her. "Although I do draw the line at anything I have to catch, scale, or skin."

Diega watched as Erin stood before the table in silence for several seconds, arms slightly out from her sides, hands spread wide.

When Erin beckoned her over, Diega asked, "Was that a blessing?"

Erin gestured at the mountains. "Who wouldn't be grateful to have a feast in these surroundings?"

Roasted chicken pieces with a crisp spinach salad, cranberry chutney, and crusty French bread was, indeed, a feast in Diega's estimation. Especially when all she had to do was consume it.

"Where did you get this? It's delicious," Diega said, licking her fingers.

"I made it. I like to cook when I have time."

"If all your efforts are like this, I'd suggest you make lots of time for cooking."

Erin took a deep breath and let it out slowly. She chewed her lower lip then said, "I really appreciate what you did for me this weekend. I don't usually..." She broke off and looked away. "I'm not much of a drinker. And I've never gotten drunk before." She gave a quick grin. "Not like that at least. I..." She stopped again and this time stared at her hands in her lap.

"You don't have to explain."

Erin looked up, but Diega could see that her focus was far from the reds and oranges of the sunset glowing across the hilltop. "I had just gotten some disturbing news. Obviously, I didn't handle it well." Her eyes seemed to readjust and take in her surroundings again. "Getting into an accident or being picked up for drunk driving would have been the perfectly awful ending for a perfectly dreadful day." She gave Diega a rueful smile. "Thanks for preventing that."

"Glad I was there."

Erin crooked her head to one side. "I thought maybe I'd run into you someday at one of the places around town."

"It's weird that you did. I'm not into the bar scene. I tend to be much more of a homebody."

"Home alone type?"

It was Diega's turn to be reticent. "At the moment." She switched the subject. "What did you tell your parents about Saturday?"

"The truth. Or, at least, most of it. I might have edited the amount of alcohol consumed."

"Your folks know that you're gay?"

Erin nodded. "I came out to them when I was in grad school. Katie and I were a newly-minted couple and I was determined to be out and proud. We each told our parents soon after. We had vowed to get ourselves to Washington D.C. for the March for Gay and Lesbian Rights in '93, and we didn't want our families to find out about us on the evening news." She kicked her boot against the picnic table leg. "Funny, that was only five years ago and yet it seems a lifetime."

As a veteran of both the '87 and '93 marches, Diega was glad the young woman had gotten to experience the high of one of those weekends, but she also knew coming out stories were rarely, if ever, totally positive. "How did your parents take it?"

"Not well at first. Disappointed. Upset. Worried what the neighbors would think. The whole nine yards." Erin shrugged. "Then they started worrying about my future. Seems they didn't think corporate America was ready for an out lesbian even if she had an MBA from Stanford. But they were wrong. I got a great job with a generous salary and they calmed down. They even unbent enough to be stiffly polite to Katie." Erin's eyes took on a wistful look. "My dad is much better about everything now. When Katie and I split, he did bring up the idea that I might like to try dating men again now that I got this 'Katie thing' out of my system." She snorted. "Maybe he'll never get it, but at least he backed off when I explained the facts of life to him. My mom is the one who still gets exasperated with me. I think we're too much alike."

"Impulsive?"

"And passionate." Erin snapped her teeth shut as if to prevent further words from escaping. She rose and started packing the remains of their repast.

Erin swung her pack over her left arm. The strap fell so that her right arm could not bend around her back quite far enough to snag it. Diega grabbed the strap and helped Erin into it. As Erin adjusted the straps, Diega lifted one of them and brushed some of Erin's hair out of the way. Erin's eyes searched Diega's face and Diega found her hand lingering in Erin's hair.

Diega pulled her hand back more abruptly than called for and cleared her throat. "Why don't we take a turn around the water tower on the hill before heading back down?"

"It's a deal."

Before they could start off, Diega's cell phone rang, destroying the illusion of being far from the reaches of civilization. She cursed mildly as she searched her pocket for the device, ruing her decision to enter the instant-access world. Sometimes, she thought as she flipped it open and pressed the answer key, not being reachable was a good thing.

Tully's twang sang across the airwaves. "I heard a newsflash on the radio. The police have a break in the murder."

Diega listened to Tully's report with more than dismay. When she hung up, she noticed Erin looking at her quizzically. Diega cleared her throat. "The police have announced that your mom is a 'person of interest' in Zeke's murder."

Chapter Thirteen

"NO WAY," ERIN said, her eyes now resembling the icy blue of an Alaskan glacier. "No frigging way. My mother did not kill that man."

Diega threw her hands out wide. "I'm not saying she did. But there must be some reason the police are questioning her. As much as I'm not a fan of the Glendale PD, they do tend to operate with evidence, not gut feelings."

"Well then," Erin said, tightening her backpack, "we'll just have to get new evidence, won't we?"

Diega heard the "we" with mixed emotions. Did Erin really mean to include her or was it a figure of speech? And did she really want to get mixed up with a murder investigation again? Especially when she was not all that fond of Sally? Maybe it would be easier when her own neck was not in the noose. With a sigh tinged with inevitability, Diega grabbed her own backpack and followed Erin down the hill.

"Do you have some plan of attack," she asked Erin's back, "or are you merely going to break your mother out of jail?"

Erin shifted her pack on her shoulders and marched onward.

After five minutes of this silent treatment, Diega sprinted forward and grabbed Erin's arm. "I am not the enemy," Diega said when Erin turned to face her. Diega noticed Erin's clenched jaw. "You don't have to shut me out."

Erin continued to glare. "I've learned that I don't have time to listen to people who tell me something can't be done. If that's how you feel, then get the hell out of my way and let me do it."

"I never said your mom is guilty. I never said anything about not being able to prove that. I was reminding you of the very inconvenient fact that the police are not going to listen to impassioned pleas." Diega took a breath, then said, "The first thing you need to do for your mom is get her a good defense lawyer. The second thing we'll need to do is decide how we can prove Sally didn't do this."

Erin nodded. "Defense lawyer, then a plan." She thought for a moment. "Where in the world do you find a defense lawyer? Yellow pages?"

"Unfortunately, I know one." At Erin's raised eyebrows, Diega waved a hand. "Don't ask, but I'll call her now."

"Thanks." Erin gave a quick grin. "I'm told I tend to be a bit prickly."

"I never would have guessed."

A breeze pushed tendrils of curls across Erin's face. Diega smothered an impulse to reach out and once again tuck them back into place. Instead she reached for her cell phone and dialed Evie's number.

"A COUNCIL OF war," Tully said with unconcealed delight.

"More of a brainstorming session, I hope," Diega said.

When Erin and Diega had arrived at the Glendale police department with defense attorney Marsha in tow, Sally Nelson had refused all help. She would not talk with her daughter and, when finally released, refused to consult with Marsha regarding any possible future actions.

When Diega called Erin later, Erin sounded confused, angry, and irritated. Her mother had completely stifled any discussion of why the police had questioned her and why they had released her. Instead, her mother headed upstairs and went to bed.

Erin seemed so distraught that Diega decided to call her friends and see if they could think of something to do. As Diega knew they would, Tully, Jenny, and Felicia gathered at her house that evening armed with desserts and questions.

Felicia and Jenny curled up on the denim couch. Sherwood brushed her whole body against their legs and looked over her shoulder at them, blinking her blue eyes beseechingly, but the two women only absently patted her head.

Sherwood finally gave up her quest for attention from the couch couple and stretched out on Tully who was spread out along the matching loveseat, booted feet on the distressed pine coffee table.

Diega had written an outline of what she felt were the salient points. She breathed deeply and, referring to her notes to keep her on track, reported on all that she knew or guessed at regarding Zeke Chambers and his death. "So," Diega finished, "I don't know if my principal killed him or not, but several things don't makes sense if she's the one."

Jenny sighed so deeply that Sherwood looked up from her perch on Tully's legs to stare up at the strange sound. "I take it this means you're off and running again. You want to investigate this."

Diega threw up her hands. "Frankly, I don't know what I want to do. I hate that the police seem to have something to tie me to this, but at least I'm only one of the suspects now. I still feel like I should do something. What that might be is anyone's guess. I suppose that's really why I asked you guys here. To get some direction."

Jenny propped her chin on her hand. Her dimples disappeared. "The police don't really seem to be targeting you anymore, so your concern about protecting your own well-being doesn't cut it, my friend. I know you don't like your principal, so I can't see that saving her hide is a huge incentive for you. That only leaves the daughter." She squinted at Diega. "So, has the recluse finally come out of her cave?"

Diega rolled her eyes. "Oh, please. Erin and I have gone hiking. We've talked. That's it. She seems like a nice kid and she's upset that her mom is being targeted. So I want to help. End of story."

"Girlfriend, I hope it's the end of the story, 'cause you better watch your back if you're even thinking of taking up with the principal's daughter." Felicia waved a finger back and forth. "You know how those teachers love to gossip. They'll be gunning for you. And what if the news got out to the parents of your kids? You might lose your job."

Diega raised her own fingers and started ticking off points. "First of all, the district can't fire me for being gay anymore. Secondly, most of the faculty already know I'm gay. Admittedly, a few of them have been less than friendly since I showed up to the faculty Christmas party with a female companion, but those people are no great loss. Most importantly, though, I'm not looking to date Erin, so all the things you're worried about aren't going to happen."

Tully thumped her boots to the wood floor causing Sherwood to leap off. She swished her tail and marched back to the couch. "Maybe Jenny's right that you might have left out one or two reasons for sticking your nose into this particular can of worms, but I'm still thinking you won't rest easy until you do something."

Felicia nodded. "Amen, sister. But, Dee, honey, this problem is not something you can solve by calling a protest march, much as I know you love to do such things. And rather than have you all by your lonesome picking through those worms that Tully mentioned, I think we need to help."

Jenny groaned and scooped up Sherwood from the floor. "I think I'm outvoted. Just tell me which hospital I need to visit your broken bodies in."

For the first time in many days, Diega relaxed.

Tully chomped on one of the oatmeal raisin cookies Felicia had brought. After she brushed the crumbs off her ample bosom, she said, "You know your district sent Zeke to deal with Gwen's company. Maybe he was refusing to help Gwen or maybe Gwen tried to bribe him and he threatened to report her. If he was trouble, then she might be tempted to bash his little head in."

Felicia shook her head. "Bears don't kill the bees, even when they're annoying. They simply take the honey. If Zeke wasn't willing to help Gwen's company, they'd find someone else. I think we should check out his amorous connections. Find out who that sweet young thing was that Zeke was escorting around the casinos."

Ignoring the voice that kept a calorie count in her head, Diega selected her favorite cookie, peanut butter with actual peanuts in it. She held it up and said, "This whole thing is nuts." From the confused faces that greeted her pronouncement, Diega felt impelled to explain. "The whole murder scene is crazy. Why murder someone at an elementary school? Why should he bleed in one room and be killed in another? And why was he even in that wing of the school? If he was meeting someone, it wasn't Sally. He and Sally always met in her office. And if he were meeting anyone else, why did they pick my hallway to meet in?"

Jenny rubbed her jaw. "Maybe he was on his way to the principal's office when someone intercepted him. Some angry someone."

Diega nodded. "The only person I've seen who fits the angry role is Zeke's son, but he could kill his father anywhere. Why would he pick the school?"

"To draw suspicion away from the family?" Jenny offered, picking up a cookie of her own.

Tubby Beelzebub strolled up to Tully and meowed. Tully picked up BB and placed the dark cat on her generous lap. BB plowed her head into Tully's stomach before flopping over on her back, presenting her own bulging belly for rubbing. "Business. Family. Girlfriends. Poker. That's a whole herd of cattle to brand. Maybe I can poke around those card clubs. A few of my compatriots like to spend time in the casinos. I could follow up on what you and your uncle found out about his high-flying wagering. See if the unlamented Zeke was flush or maybe borrowing cash on his good looks. Maybe even pick up some dope about the mysterious man in black."

Diega shook her head. "That guy is scary. I really don't want you messing with him."

"Moi?" Tully said, fluttering her long eyelashes. "Why would you think I'd do something foolish like that?"

Felicia shook her head and cast her eyes to the ceiling. "You can always tell a Texan..." Jenny and Diega joined her for the ending, "...but you can't tell her much."

Jenny hoisted her elegant, long legs onto Diega's coffee table. Her eyes swept over Diega before resting on Tully. "No offense, but what are you planning on doing with whatever information is gathered? You two have a history of getting yourselves into activities that haven't exactly been good for any of your friends' blood pressure." Turning to Diega she added, "And, in case you've forgotten, Felicia and I have a moving date coming up and I'd like you two to be physically fit enough to help with the hauling."

Diega said reassuringly, "Tully and I have learned our lessons. I promise. All information will be passed to Detective Theophilus as soon as we've verified it."

Jenny's eyebrow reached for her hairline. "Do I sense a little wiggle room there?"

Diega cleared her throat and changed the topic. "I'm going to call Gwen Gunther. She wanted to talk with me anyway about a charter school her company is trying to open. Since she's dealing with the district, maybe she can give me some news on Zeke."

Felicia pulled herself out of Jenny's protective arm and sat up. "Where did this guy live?"

Surprised by the question, Diega nevertheless answered, "North Glendale. Above the country club. Why?"

"Did his wife match their house?"

"If you mean did she look like money, yes. More than Zeke actually."

"In that case," Felicia said, "there are only a couple of salons where she'd get her hair done. I have a few sisters who work in that area. Let me get the stylists' underground working on the family angle."

Jenny sighed. "I might as well check with my buddy in law enforcement. Even though Zeke's family is in Glendale, maybe the LAPD has something on the errant son."

"Could you also check on Zeke's previous employment? I'm wondering if someone from the past might have it out for him."

"Oh, sure. I only have to clear out an entire room, empty a closet, and make room in my den for Felicia's haircutting chair and equipment all in the next two weeks. I've got plenty of time to do some detective work." With a sigh and a head shake, Jenny dutifully grabbed a sheet of paper to jot down her assignment. "By the way. This means you'll be getting back most of the furniture you lent me when I moved in. You may have to do some weeding yourself."

Diega grinned. "Have I told you guys lately that I love you?"

FELICIA AND JENNY left, pleading a need to continue packing. Tully stayed on, telling Diega they had to talk. "Compared with the excitement of your week," Tully said, sipping some decaf coffee, "planning a party for the soon-to-be U-Hauled isn't quite the thrill it could have been, but we do need to get started."

"Oh, yes. Death and destruction always outshine cohabitation."

Diega thought of Tully's ongoing parade of female companions, most of whom were charming, intelligent, and exceptionally good-looking. None of whom lasted more than a few months. Except one.

"Will you be bringing Gina to this event?" Diega asked, referring to the one and only long-lasting relationship of Tully's love life, an LAPD detective.

Tully picked at some lint on her sleeve. "Probably. Even though love and marriage aren't high on her hit parade at the moment."

Diega figured Tully was referring to the protracted divorce proceedings Gina had been struggling with for over six months. "I wondered since I didn't see her at the party Sunday."

"She had the weekend off so she took her son to visit her parents in Reno. They left right after David got out of school Friday." Tully stretched and yawned. "And which of your many lovelies might you be bringing along?"

Diega answered Tully's yawn with one of her own. It had been a long week and it was only Tuesday. "There's nobody I'd want to invite to this. When you invite someone to a wedding or a commitment ceremony or whatever, it kind of means more. It's not a casual date. And there's nobody that fits that bill at the moment."

"There's been nobody to fit that bill since Evie. Isn't it about time to take another jump into that big, beautiful pool of vulnerability named relationship?"

Diega gave a scornful laugh. "A lecture on the joys of matrimony from a monk."

Tully raised an eyebrow, but switched the subject. "Did I tell you my tenants have moved out?"

Diega blinked at the change of subject. "Really? You had them quite a while. Do you want me to put a rental notice on the bulletin board at school?"

"No, thanks. I'm actually going to move into it myself."

Diega was shocked. Tully had owned a three-bedroom home in Silver Lake for as long as Diega had known her. And she had always rented it out. Tully had frequently proclaimed that she preferred apartment living since it allowed her freedom to roam with no maintenance worries.

Diega nudged Tully with her foot. "I'm having trouble picturing you mowing a lawn."

"That's what a checkbook is for. But it does have a great backyard. It would be nice for David to have a place to play outside."

This time Diega's jaw dropped. "David? As in Gina's son?" Tully was renowned for a dislike of anyone under the age of twenty-five.

Tully shrugged. "Since the divorce, they've been in an apartment. Not much of a life for a twelve-year-old."

Diega gave Tully a wicked grin. "Maybe Gina could get a good deal if she shared Felicia's moving van."

Tully choked on her coffee and steered the conversation back to the party.

Their discussion continued into the late hours, with Diega in the boring and unfamiliar position of naysayer. Diega had to admit that Tully's ideas—ranging from a circus spectacular with Felicia and Jenny each riding into center ring on elephants to a midnight horseback ride through Griffith Park—all had entertainment value, but she thought it her duty to protect her friends from embarrassment, discomfort, and possible bankruptcy.

Diega extended a plain wrap suggestion. "Why don't we have a backyard barbeque? We could string up lights like they did last night and maybe even put down a dance floor. Your Silver Lake place would be perfect for it."

The look of pity that lit upon Tully face would have been appropriate if Diega had announced she had a week to live. "Dee, these are our best friends. If they are silly enough to take themselves out of the market and hole up together for the rest of their lives, we have to give them something to tell their grandchildren about."

"I'm not sure grandchildren are part of the picture just yet."

"You never know. Why should straight people get all the misery? I say we should go out and breed. We couldn't do any worse than some of those so-called natural parents."

"That reminds me," Diega said, thinking of a conversation she had had with Matt Hunter, a fellow Glendale teacher, at Jenny and Felicia's party. He had told Diega that Zeke had two sons, one seventeen and one eleven, both now attending a private school. Diega filled Tully in on her leap in subject matter. "Matt said the one we met—you know, Mr. Motorcycle Wayne—has been in trouble with the police. A lot of juvenile stuff, but he also got expelled for bringing a knife to school."

"A knife? Like in the implement used on your custodian? And Zeke was stabbed as well. How very interesting." Tully fingered her chin. "Sounds like sonny boy has anger issues galore. Makes you wonder what kind of a father Zeke was."

"I don't know. I'm beginning to wonder how much I knew about Zeke at all." Diega poured them each another cup of coffee. "Theophilus made me think about why Zeke was willing to risk his career to give me information the union could use against the district. I didn't even question it at the time. Do you think Zeke could have been playing me? What if the numbers he gave me aren't right? Could he have been setting up the union for some reason?"

Tully rocked on the back legs of her chair. "Seems like something to check out before marching into the next session with possibly shaky facts. Thing is, why would he do that?"

"Don't know." Diega stared blankly ahead for several seconds. "Some things are really not adding up. Like, I wonder how Zeke managed to support an expensive private school, that home of his, and gambling."

Tully took another swig of coffee before responding. "Sounds like you're ready to saddle up and ride after the horse thieves." She broke into a grin. "You'd better remember I'd be mighty put out if you were off sleuthing without me."

Chapter Fourteen

DETECTIVE THEOPHILUS WAITED outside Diega's room when she arrived Wednesday morning. All cheerful thoughts of parties and lessons fled her head and the frustrations of the last several days took their place.

"Look," Diega said, wrenching the door open and slamming on the lights, "you've already dragged Sally in for questioning. Why are you bothering me again?" She tossed her purse and file folder on the desk where they landed with a thud.

"And just so you know," Diega said, gathering steam, "if you think Zeke was in my room it could explain a little item you have against me. You know those strands of hair that Zeke had that are supposedly mine? Were they cut or did they have the roots attached?"

The detective's silence pushed Diega to continue. "The only scenario I can see that would explain him having a handful of my hair is if we struggled. If we had, he would have torn the hair from my head and the roots would still be attached. However," Diega said, in her best lecture tones, "if those hairs were cut, he wouldn't have them as a result of a fight. So, if they are cut, and if they are truly mine, there's only one place he might have gotten them."

Diega waited for an excited question or even a polite grunt of interest. All she got was his breathing. "Where, you might ask? Even though you haven't, I'll tell you." She pointed a finger to the back of her room. "My science center. I had samples of various animal hairs, including my own. And when I got back into my room Friday morning I noticed the dish with my hair in it was almost empty."

"We noticed that, too."

Diega felt her moment of shining detection being blown away.

Theophilus continued. "Which brings us to another point. If those hairs came from your science center, then when was he in your classroom and why? Also, how did he get in here since he didn't have a key and you claim you didn't let him in. And why might he fool around with your science display?" He cleared his throat. "I'm open to suggestions."

"All the suggestions I have for you are rude."

Theophilus burst into laughter. After several moments he regained control. "You are quite a feisty woman. I really hope I don't have to arrest you for murder." He shook his head. "By the way, the reason I stopped by was because I thought you should know that Luis Hernandez has been upgraded from critical to serious. He's still in a coma, but they're saying his chances of pulling through are much better."

DIEGA'S DAY IMPROVED once the detective left. After class, she packed up hurriedly knowing she had a dinner meeting with Gwen Gunther. Unfortunately, Megan Beaker entered her classroom before Diega had a chance to escape. The motor in Megan's mouth had revived and was now revved high. "Diega! I got some new materials for a unit on the California missions!" She gushed forth facts, figures, fancies, and whatever else her eyes and mind lit upon. As she spoke she wandered around the room, picking up objects and moving displays around.

Reminding herself of her mentoring duties, Diega asked, "Is there something I can help you with?"

"Not really. I have a meeting with a parent in a little bit and when I saw you were still here I thought I'd stop by and say hi," she said, plopping down in a student's chair. She leapt back up. "Ugh. What is this?" Chocolate blobs, remnants of illicit treats, discolored both sleeves where she had laid them on the desk.

Diega pointed at the sink. "Wash it off now before it stains."

"I thought your sink was broken. Didn't you come into my room and borrow water the other day?" A blast of water gushed forth when she turned the faucet handle. "I see they fixed it. Of course I don't know if water will take out a chocolate stain. Oh well, if this doesn't come off, I'll walk home and change before the meeting. It only takes five minutes. You know I only live a few blocks over." Megan's mouth was off and running again even as she scrubbed her sleeves at the sink.

Diega's ears ignored most of Megan's chatter until two familiar names broke through the blockade. "What about Zeke and Sally?"

Megan shook her hands before grabbing a paper towel to dry them and blot her sleeve. "I only meant I saw you talking with that policeman so many times, I thought you'd know if they'd checked into what I told them."

"So you decided to go to the police?"

Megan's eyes grew wide. "Oh, no. It's not like that at all. The detective came to me and asked me if I'd ever seen Zeke at school before and I mentioned that I had heard that he came around a lot this year to see Sally and—"

Diega held up her hand. To her surprise, she found herself defending Sally. "Sally is our principal and a married woman. If you have some evidence," Diega said, putting emphasis on the word, "then tell the police. But gossip doesn't help anyone—and it might ruin some reputations, not to mention waste police time."

Megan stuck out her chin. "This is not gossip. I saw him in her office one morning and they certainly looked very cozy. Especially for two married people."

"When was this?"

Megan pulled her hair over one shoulder and ran her fingers through it. "A couple of days before he died. I remember because that was the first day of teaching my class our dance for the Spring Festival and I needed to borrow the portable microphone from the office." She tapped Diega on her shoulder. "Imagine my surprise when Sally's door was open and there was Zeke leaning over her." She frowned. "I never did get the microphone. I had to yell over the boom box. I nearly lost my voice."

GWEN GUNTHER HAD sounded pleased when Diega called to arrange a dinner together. They met at a coffee shop in Glendale where Gwen grabbed a booth for four so she would have room to spread out brochures and documents regarding her company.

"Charter schools are relatively new, but I think they can be a great alternative for students, parents, and teachers," Gwen explained as she buttered a roll and pointed to a fact sheet with her elbow.

As Diega sipped her soup, Gwen went on to explain how the rules and administration differed for her schools. "So you see we really listen to the community and to the teachers. It's not a top-down organization. You'd be your own boss in so many ways. And if you wanted to take on the lead instructor position, you'd have a half-time load and a say in the running of the school. Everything from curriculum to textbooks would be your baby."

By now the main courses had arrived. Diega twirled her spaghetti as she considered Gwen's offer. To be her own boss was tempting as was the loosening of restriction on what she could teach and when. It would afford her the freedom to do creative units with her students, allowing them to showcase their talents outside of traditional academics. "What about standardized tests?"

Gwen sighed. "We still have to give them and we report our scores. But," she said, in a brighter tone, "we're betting that when we hire good teachers and let them decide how to teach their own students, the scores will go up. We also require involvement from the parents. It's definitely a group effort."

Diega considered a piece of garlic bread, but resisted, knowing she would have to jog an extra five miles the next morning to make up for it. "So you cherry-pick the most involved families and dump the students whose parents who don't know enough to be active in their education or who are working so much that they can't take part."

"We don't dump students. Anyone who applies is admitted. If we have too many applicants, we have to hold a lottery. And all families are eligible to apply for the lottery."

"So what happens to the kids whose parents don't know enough to apply for the lottery? Or the ones who don't know how the system works, so they never even consider alternatives for their kids?"

Gwen sighed. "If you can figure out how to reach those families, please let me know. Together we could make a mint."

Diega decided that antagonizing Gwen was not going to do her any good. She switched to neutral ground. "Do you have competition for setting up charter schools or is each district the exclusive purview of a company?"

"Any group can form a charter school. In fact, there's a new one on the scene called Education Edge that's bidding for opening a series of schools including one in Glendale. But they have no track record, so I think we have a better chance of convincing the teachers and Board that our vision will serve the students best."

"I'd want to visit one of your schools before seriously talking about a job with your company."

Gwen was more than willing for Diega to visit as many campuses and talk to as many people as she wanted.

Diega thought it was time to steer the conversation to Zeke, if possible. "Is this the pitch you gave the Glendale USD?"

"I haven't met with your Board yet. I've only talked with your superintendent and he passed me off to his assistant. You know, the one who was killed." Gwen shook her head, though whether from sorrow or disgust, Diega could not tell.

"So you actually worked with Zeke?"

"It was more like Zeke tried to work me. I felt like I was giving him more information than I was getting." Gwen leaned forward. "I'm hoping he wasn't indicative of your top administration. He was out for himself first, last, and everywhere in between."

"How so?"

Gwen surveyed the room before answering. "Let's just say, he was willing to support our proposal, but only for a price. A very steep price."

Chapter Fifteen

"GOOD THING YOU had those insurance figures," Jim said as he and Diega headed into the union hall after the morning negotiation session. "Who knew the district was hiding rebates from the insurance companies? Wouldn't the administration be embarrassed if the press got hold of that little gem? That bomb sure made them a little more amenable to our proposals, wouldn't you say?"

Diega recognized Jim's feeling of triumph, but inside she only felt relief. She had not been able to verify all of the facts Zeke had given her. The few they used had been enough to move the administration at the table. She still did not trust that everything Zeke had told her was accurate, but the fact that some were made her wonder anew at his motives. Had he been trying to make the district look bad? What would that gain him?

Diega headed to the water cooler to refill her glass. She felt a hand on her shoulder and turned to face a short, stocky African-American man who grinned at her with delight.

"Diega!" the man shouted and wrapped his arms around her.

Diega tried to extract her upper body with minimal bruising. Lloyd Michaels was a fellow teacher in Glendale, although he had the fortitude to work with students in the full throes of puberty, otherwise known as high school.

Lloyd and Diega had met seven years ago at a union function. Both of them were flirting with the same woman who was encouraging them equally. When they finally figured out what was happening, Diega and Lloyd had dropped their pursuit of the woman and headed to the bar together to split a pitcher of beer.

Diega asked, "What are you doing here?"

"Released time for a grievance case. I'm the union rep for our school. And you?"

"Released for negotiations. Supposed to be all day, but now I think I might have a free afternoon. We kind of kicked the feet out from under the district this morning."

Lloyd pulled Diega to the side of the room and lowered his voice. "I heard that you were found standing over Zeke's body, bloody knife in hand. You should have called me. I'd have come over and helped." He dropped his voice even lower. "The rumor mill is saying that the police are asking mighty pointed questions about you and Zeke."

Diega did not bother to correct the gossip.

Lloyd shook his head sadly. "The thing is, the police are looking in all the wrong places."

"Where should they be looking?"

Lloyd looked around before answering. "You know Zeke was the superintendent's fair-haired boy. Whatever he suggested seemed to go sailing through. Well, Zeke's the one who sold the district on Brighter Days."

Diega knew that Brighter Days was a private "credit recovery" program that the district had teamed with. The program provided high school students an opportunity to make up any credits they needed to graduate. The idea was that the graduation rate would increase. She had heard that the district and the private company would split the amount of state revenues generated by the hours of attendance.

Lloyd shook his head. "Nobody asked the teachers about the deal. I checked it out once they got the program up and running." He blew air out of his cheeks. "The curriculum is shaky and the kids are getting credit for sitting in front of a school computer with generic software and pushing buttons for four hours a day. What kind of education is that?"

"No one examined the curriculum before they hired the company?"

Lloyd shook his head. "Brighter Days waved money and the district came running."

"I'm surprised the school board isn't all over this."

"Zeke vouched for both the program and the company so the board asked no questions." Lloyd smiled grimly. "Rumor has it that Brighter Days has an executive VP position coming up offering a high six figure salary. Want to guess who the number one contender is, or rather, was?"

SINCE THE DISTRICT cancelled afternoon negotiations to regroup, BB and Sherwood had the unexpected pleasure of Diega's company at home. Her early arrival did not deter them from demanding food, no matter how earnestly Diega explained that one o'clock was not the dinner hour.

The doorbell interrupted the family dispute. Erin stood on the front step. Surprise and pleasure vied in Diega's mind as she invited the young woman inside.

"Sorry to barge in. I heard that you might be home and I thought I'd take a chance." Erin shoved her hands in her back pockets. "I'm feeling antsy and my parents are driving me crazy. So I wondered if you might like a short hike in the hills. I heard about an easy trail that's near the Angeles Crest Highway."

More than willing to be distracted, Diega said, "Let me feed my girls and change."

The drive to the nearby mountains took half an hour. During the trip, neither one mentioned Zeke, Luis, or anything else having to do with Vista Elementary. Instead talk revolved around music, movies, and outdoor activities.

They parked on the side of the road near the trailhead. Diega noticed a Montrose Search and Rescue truck parked farther up. Knowing it meant some poor hiker was lost or injured, she said, "I hope that isn't a sign. Maybe we'd better bring extra food and water."

Even though the Verdugo Mountains and the Angeles Crest Forest were the backyard of Burbank, Diega was only vaguely familiar with the roads and trails that meandered through the wilderness. She had hiked some of the most commonly used trails, but the one Erin was leading her along was an unfamiliar one. The dirt path felt remote, but an occasional engine rumble told Diega that the highway was just up the incline from them.

Pine trees and scrub oak lined the hillsides. Their boots caused dust to puff up around their feet with every step. The hem of Diega's jeans were becoming thick with the powdery dirt. She called a halt to take a swig of water and to beat the legs of her pants clean.

Erin took the opportunity to whack her own boots against a rock. "I'm going to take a wild guess and say it hasn't rained lately."

"Rain? You mean that myth that water falls from the sky?" Diega stomped her shoes. "As a ninth-generation native Californian, I can assure you that rain thing is a story made up by the government to take people's minds off UFOs."

Erin smiled, but the look faded quickly from her face. She turned away, but not before Diega caught the look of pain that replaced Erin's smile.

Diega felt her heart hurt for the young woman. She reached over and cupped Erin's chin, forcing Erin to look at her. "What's wrong? Is it your mom or is something else going on?" She dropped her hand. "Want to talk?"

Erin locked eyes with Diega. "I really wish I had met you at another time in my life. You're funny and fun and beautiful. I felt drawn to you the first time I saw you in my mom's office."

Unable to read Erin's eyes and unable to filter her own emotions, Diega settled for an attempt at humor. "And that's a bad thing?"

The brief smile flitted over Erin's face again.

Before Erin could respond, Diega held up a hand. She heard a mewling sound, as if an animal was injured or crying for its mother. She waved at Erin and said, "Listen."

Both women stood silently. The quiet keen turned to a groan.

Diega started toward the sound, but Erin caught her sleeve. "Injured animals can be dangerous."

"At least we should check to see what it is so that we can report it."

Erin shook her head, but followed as Diega crept to the edge of the trail where the distressed sounds seemed to be originating. At this point, the hillside was steep. Only some boulders and a few scraggly bushes jutted out from the scree to keep it from being a free fall to the bottom of the canyon. Among the grey rocks and brown bramble, Diega saw the blue of a leg encased in jeans.

"It's a person," she said to Erin. "Here's my phone. Call 911. I'll see if there's a safe way down to them."

Diega searched the edge of the hillside for some footholds. Several rocks looked promising, but when she put her foot on them, they crumbled or slid out from the dirt and tumbled twenty feet down the embankment.

Erin called out. "There's no cell phone reception up here. I'm going to hike back to the road and see if I can find someone from that search and rescue unit." She moved to stand beside Diega and peered over the cliff. "I've done some rappelling and I wouldn't try this cliff without gear. Why don't you just wait until I come back with some help?"

A long, rattling moan echoed up from the figure below, then silence.

"I don't know if they can wait that long." Diega scanned the edge in both directions. She pointed. "Look. There's space between those lower boulders. I bet I could slide down the crack and that would land me close by."

Erin gave Diega a dubious look, then headed down the trail at a run.

Diega scrambled over two large sandstone boulders and found herself on a narrow outcropping. From there, she leapt to the top of the next large rock. She then lowered herself carefully over the side of it and landed on the rounded top of one of the boulders she had spotted from the trail. The flattened ledge of that boulder was roughly two feet across. Diega inched across to this landing and breathed heavily. It was only then that she considered that the sheriff's department may end up rescuing two people instead of only one if she couldn't find a way down to the victim from her current perch.

Diega lay across the narrow edge and peered over. She could see the person's body more clearly now. The blue jeans led to a filthy and torn plaid shirt which was twisted around a bruised and bloodied male body. As she watched, the individual's chest rose and shuddered. A quiet groan emanated from him.

At the sound, Diega swung her body around to where the two boulders almost touched. The crack between the rocks was narrow, but she wedged herself into it and slowly slid her way down to the victim.

Diega knew she had to check for signs of responsiveness first. She lightly shook the man. "Hey, guy. Can you hear me?"

No response greeted Diega's effort. The man's breathing was shallow and irregular and Diega had difficulty finding a pulse. She brushed away leaves and debris that covered his face and part of his chest in order to determine if CPR was needed.

Harrison Carter, science teacher and poker junkie, lay revealed.

Stunned, Diega momentarily forgot her rescue mission.

Erin's voice echoed down the hillside. "How is he?"

Jolted into action, Diega checked for obvious bleeding or broken bones. "He's unresponsive. He's breathing, but just barely. No obvious broken bones. I think he cracked his head, but the bleeding seems to have stopped. His skin is really cold. I don't know if he's in shock or if he's been here all night."

"That's a great report."

The sound of a male's voice made Diega look up. A man in a sheriff's uniform peered down at her.

"If you have any extra clothes, cover him. Otherwise, sit still and we'll get a litter down there to get you both up."

Diega looked along the ridge in amazement. "Good grief. Do you have an office on the trail or what? How did you get here so fast?"

"We're up here on another call. Lost hiker. Since we haven't found him yet, we'll take care of your guy first." The radio on his hip crackled. He grabbed it and spoke for several seconds. He yelled down to Diega, "Air 5 should be here any minute. Now get him warmed up."

Diega stripped off her light jacket and draped it over Harrison. She pulled out the bottom of her T-shirt and used it to wipe the dirt from his face. His cleaner face revealed bruises and swellings. To Diega they looked more like the result of a beating than of a fall.

The thudding of a helicopter's blades sounded in the distance, then rapidly grew louder. As Diega looked up, two people wearing backpacks descended from the helicopter, dangling on the end of a winch cable. They had gear dripping from every loop on their packs and a litter trapped between them.

They landed on a ledge to the right of where Diega and Harrison perched. One of the people waved the copter off while the other, a woman, yelled over to Diega. "Montrose Search and Rescue here. We'll take over now."

BY LATE THAT afternoon Harrison Carter looked more colorful in many ways. The bruising on his face and arms had reached the puce purple swelling stage. His skin tone was healthier, showing some pink instead of cadaverous white.

Diega slid a chair to his hospital bedside. "I know you don't believe this, but you look better."

Harrison swiveled his eyes in her direction. "You're right. I don't," he mumbled from between swollen lips.

Diega thought she detected a tooth or two missing, but decided not to ask. "So who did this to you?"

Harrison's eyes flickered away. "I fell."

And I'm Harry Potter, Diega thought. "You go hiking often?"

"First time."

"Well, then, let me tell you. Next time you might want to take a backpack and some water and maybe even wear something other than dress shoes."

Harrison stared straight ahead.

"Harrison, I was at the club the night you got into a fight with that man in black. I know he's a loan shark. Are you in hock to him?"

Harrison closed his eyes.

Undeterred, Diega pressed. "You accused him of being a murderer. Did you mean Zeke's murder?"

A snort came from the bed.

"Harrison, I'm on your side. I want to make sure that whoever hurt you doesn't hurt anyone else. Trust me on this."

The red lights on the bedside monitor blinked off and on silently for several minutes before Harrison slowly turned his head toward her. "Unless you're Superwoman in disguise, there's nothing you can do to stop Carl."

"That the guy in black?"

Harrison nodded.

"What's his last name?"

A noncommittal shrug followed by a groan.

"How was Zeke involved with Carl? Was Carl Zeke's big backer?"

Harrison snorted again and looked to the ceiling. As Diega was about to give up and leave he muttered, "You've got it all backward. Zeke bankrolled Carl."

Chapter Sixteen

"ACCORDING TO HARRISON, Zeke suddenly stopped supplying funds to Carl and Carl was none too pleased." Diega had phoned Tully as soon as she had gotten into her car. "Carl had to use his own money to front these loans and the terms got less generous, one may say."

"So where did our dearly departed get all that dough?"

"That may be the question of the hour."

"Maybe we should all go out to dinner tonight. We'll meet at your house at six."

After arriving home and feeding her two self-proclaimed starving felines a second dinner, Diega felt too restless to sit and wait for her friends. To distract herself from dwelling on her aborted conversation with Erin, she wandered into her front yard and noticed that her flowerbeds looked dry.

Diega laid the hose in her nascent rose garden and turned on the water to a trickle. As she straightened she saw her neighbor, Amelia Holmes, leaning on her cane by her own lush bed of roses.

Diega called to her. "Hey, Mrs. Holmes. I was thinking about planting some vegetables in the backyard. Any suggestions?"

Amy Holmes grunted as she spread pellets of plant food onto the soil around her roses. "You better take care of your roses first, young lady, or you won't have blooms worth the water you're using on the plants."

Used to her neighbor's acerbic ways, Diega ignored the comment and offered to help mix the organic food into the soil. Since Mrs. Holmes gave her flowers to her son's upscale restaurant that used them to make rose-flavored sorbet, she was careful to use only natural material on her plants. Diega was trying to model her own garden on Mrs. Holmes's eco-friendly habits.

Mrs. Holmes supervised as Diega worked the pellets into the soil. She directed Diega to a section she had missed then said, "We had a Victory Garden when I was a child."

Diega leaned back on her haunches and looked up at her neighbor. "Was that at this house?"

Mrs. Holmes nodded. "We grew most of our own vegetables. You know this whole area used to be Gene Autry's ranch? Lots of years of manure piled onto this dirt. Everyone knows Burbank soil will grow anything."

"It's good enough to overcome my black thumb." Diega said, nodding at her renovated landscaping.

Mrs. Holmes harrumphed as she scanned the rose leaves for signs of disease. She plucked off an insect, examined it, then returned it to the roses. She frowned at Diega and asked, "Are you mixed up in that murder at your school?"

Diega played with the dirt in the rose bed. "Define 'mixed up.'"

"Well, that's an answer in itself." Mrs. Holmes picked off another bug. "You know, I've seen that young man who was killed somewhere before. When they showed his picture on the news, he looked familiar. He didn't come and visit you, did he?"

"Not in this lifetime."

"It'll come to me. In the meantime, is your house safe? I'm hoping you learned something after your last adventure."

Diega cringed at her mental picture of the ransacked rooms left by a murderer three years ago. "I not only have locks and dead bolts, but security screens. Plus, I don't think I'm up for baiting anyone ever again."

Mrs. Holmes wagged her cane in Diega's face. "If you do, you'd better not leave me out of it."

"THE POSSE HAS arrived." Tully tromped into Diega's living room with Felicia and Jenny close behind. They were carrying plates of food and bowls of salad.

"I thought we were going out to dinner," Diega said, although smelling the aroma from one plate made her stomach happy about eating at home.

Felicia hugged Diega. "Girlfriend, don't you look a gift horse in the muzzle. My honey here even made one of her berry pies for the occasion."

"If Jenny baked, I'm definitely saving room for dessert."

The dining room table was rapidly set and readied for a feast that included Tully's pork barbeque and Felicia's garden salad and spicy beans as well as Jenny's pie. Diega provided sourdough rolls and opened a bottle of 1988 Cabernet for the occasion.

After the first bite of the tangy pork Diega asked, "Why the potluck?"

Tully wiped the sauce off her chin. "We thought we'd give you our investigative reports in the privacy of your own home rather than announce our results to a restaurant full of spies."

Felicia flicked her napkin at Tully. "You remind me of our old hound dog who would never bury a bone if anyone else was in sight. She'd drag the thing around with her for days until she figured it was safe. Thing is," she took a sip of wine, "she never once dug up one of those carefully hidden bones."

Diega coughed. "So other than the fact that Tully reminds you of your paranoid dog, what did you find out?"

Felicia jumped in first. She had found the hairdresser who did Mrs. Zeke Chambers's hair. Mrs. Chambers apparently loved to name drop, throw lavish parties, complain a lot, and tip poorly. "Don't women know that they get a lot more for their money when they treat people well?"

Diega said, "So the wife likes her social position. She likes to spend money. That makes four things Zeke was funding: his wife, his gambling, his loan shark business, and his son's private school."

"Five." Jenny corrected her. "You forgot their lifestyle. They not only have that house, but a vacation home in Morro Bay. But that's not all." She nudged Felicia. "Tell her what the other clients said."

"The buzz at Mary's shop—that's my friend—is that the Chambers's marriage was in trouble. They evidently argued over the kids and some of the clients say that Zeke has been fooling around on the side. One whisper is that it's his secretary, but someone else says his wife suspects a business associate."

Tully asked, "Why not boot the cheat in the backside and be done with it?"

Felicia shrugged. "Maybe they've got a prenup and she'd be left with nothing."

Diega said, "So she suspects her husband is having an affair but she doesn't know with whom. Maybe she doesn't have proof, only suspicions."

"Sounds like a motive to kill your rich husband. You get rid of the cheat and keep the dough," Jenny said.

Tully cleared her throat. "Before we settle on a motive too soon, let me throw another spin into this." She explained about finding several of Zeke's poker-playing pals. "They're not exactly on my best buddy list, but we've worked together." They all reported the same thing. Zeke liked to bet large and he always seemed to have ample cash.

Tully looked at Diega. "Knowing what you get paid, it sure does confirm Zeke baby needed a separate stream of money to keep up his standard of living."

Diega drummed her fingers on the table. "That ties in with his putting the squeeze on Gwen and the charter school group. Maybe even supports the rumor about his getting a job with the Brighter Futures Company. But would that be enough money for all he had going?"

Felicia said, "Maybe he had an inheritance or something."

"Maybe," Tully said, "but if that's the case, why all the outside enterprises?"

Diega ran her fingers through her hair. "Seems like the more we know, the more we don't know."

Jenny twirled her glass stem in her hand before raising an eyebrow at Diega. "Speaking of what we don't know, have you learned anything more from Erin?"

Diega shook her head. "She says her parents still won't talk to her about the whole thing." She played with the salad on her plate. "I keep coming back to the fact that she arrived home unexpectedly right after this whole thing happened. Why did she change her plans so suddenly? Did something her parents say to her make her think their marriage was in trouble?"

Jenny asked, "Are you sure she came home after the whole mess exploded?"

"That's what she said and I never questioned her arrival." Diega sat back. "I wonder how we could find out when she got back into the country."

Jenny said, "I already checked."

Diega looked at the others and found they were as surprised as she was.

"I have a friend who knows how to access flight rosters." Jenny held up her hand. "Don't ask me about the legalities of it. Erin Nelson arrived at LAX two days before Zeke was murdered."

Tully slapped the table. "Well I'll be a slung down saddle. That sure puts a new dark horse into the race. Doesn't seem like she'd have much of a motive, though."

"Maybe more of one than we know." Diega looked at each of her friends. "When did she learn her mother and Zeke were having an affair?"

Chapter Seventeen

MOTOR MOUTH MEGAN caught Diega as she was unlocking the door to her room. "I have a major problem. I was going to demonstrate how the lungs work, but the model the district sent doesn't have the rubber gasket in it, and Sally is supposed to come and evaluate me today, and I don't know what I can do if there's no vacuum in the jar. I mean, the lungs won't work, will they?"

Diega flipped on the light switch and slid a stack of corrected tests onto her desk. It was a struggle not to snap at Megan. This was not the first time, or even the fifth, that the new teacher had neglected to check her equipment the day before a lesson. Sighing, she put her purse into the bottom drawer then faced her nemesis. "I don't suppose you have an alternative lesson on tap."

Diega knew the answer even before Megan gave a helpless shrug. Grumbling, Diega grabbed her keys and said, "There should be some balloons left over from last year's graduation. One of those should work. I think they're in the auditorium."

The storage closet in the auditorium was locked. Diega was going to send Megan to find the temporary custodian, but Megan demurred. "I'm the one who stores all the large art supplies in this space. But I just shove things in to get them out of my classroom.. It would never occur to me that there would be balloons in here, for heaven's sake. I mean, who would put balloons in an art cupboard?" She flipped through her own large key ring as she spoke, finally producing one that worked, and the two women were soon rummaging through the stacks of boxes and broken equipment that were entombed within.

Crepe paper, large rolls of butcher paper, a cracked bat with a brown stain on one side, pieces of chairs and desks, a wicked looking pair of garden shears, and, finally, a box of party supplies.

While Megan wondered aloud which of the sizes would fit her contraption, Diega decided to grab a couple of balloons and stash them aside for a demonstration of Newton's third law of physics that would be coming up next month.

Megan's jabbering took a different turn. "Have you noticed how that detective looks at you?"

Jarred out of a mental lesson planning on equal and opposite reactions, Diega looked vaguely at Megan. "You mean Theophilus? What about him?"

Megan shook her long hair. "I don't think it's fair that you haven't told him. Of course, for some men it's a turn on." She looked at Diega speculatively. "Is that your angle? I mean I've never really seen you with a woman."

"Of all the asinine..." Diega clamped her jaw shut and whirled away. She slammed the auditorium door closed, heedless of whether or not Megan was directly behind her. She rather hoped Megan's pert nose had been smashed flat by the door.

As Diega stomped down the hallway, Jim Tolkien called out to her. "Have you seen Sally?"

Diega snapped, "I am not her goddamn keeper."

"Well aren't you Little Miss Sunshine this morning? What's eating you?"

Diega shook her head. "I'll tell you later. What's up?"

Jim groaned. "The PTA luncheon is next week and Sally hasn't done any of the things I asked her to do. It's one thing to be roped into helping her and it's another when I'm left to do everything by myself." A glimmer of hope passed over his features. "You wouldn't want to co-chair this little fête, would you?"

"Grab Rita. She loves organizing things. If anyone can pull this together, she can. And I promise to talk to Sally about the luncheon the next time I see her. In fact," she said, making a U-turn, "I think I'll see if I can track her down and talk to her now."

Diega rapped on the frame of the doorway leading into the principal's office. "Sally, I need to talk with you about Megan. I cannot mentor that woman anymore."

Sally barely looked up from the paperwork on her desk. "It's part of your contract as a mentor and a condition of your extra pay that you work with the new teachers."

"I understand that. And I'm willing to pick up another newbie. I need to get this one off my back."

The principal stood and glared at Diega. "Whatever problems you and Megan are having, you need to work out. I've got my own."

"Don't we all? But you're supposed to be in charge of this place."

A look in Sally's eye warned Diega to step back and take a breath before she said something that could get her written up for insubordination. When she was finally able to check her anger, she noticed that Sally not only had dark rings under her eyes, but her hair was brushed back rather than styled, and her clothes were not perfectly coordinated. "Jeez. You look like shit." Diega said.

Sally's head snapped up. Her glare propelled Diega two steps back.

Diega raised her hands in front of her chest. "Hey. No problem. We'll talk about this later. You obviously have a lot going on right now." She watched Sally flop back into her desk chair. "Anything I can do to help?"

"That would be a first," Sally said as she flipped through the papers on her desk, avoiding Diega's eyes. "You may think you've got some sort of personal connection with me merely because you and Erin have become friendly. But you don't, and I am certainly not going to talk to you about anything that is going on that is not school related."

Rather than retreating, Diega shut the door to the principal's office and sat down on the upholstered chair by Sally's desk. "I didn't bring it up because of Erin. I brought it up because I'm actually worried about you. As I so indelicately put it, you look like hell. You let plans for the PTA luncheon fall through, and the police are still focusing their attention on you. I'm thinking you aren't doing so well."

Sally stacked the papers she had shuffled. "Your concern is noted. Now, I have work to do, so please leave."

Diega fought the urge to do just that. "Look, you're not doing your job right now, and it's pissing off some of the faculty. That is really not something you want to do." She leaned forward. "I've been the number one suspect in a murder investigation. It's no fun. You need all the help you can get, even from people you don't want involved."

Sally slammed her palms on the desktop and stood, staring down at Diega. "I know you consider yourself an expert in teaching merely because you wrangled a mentor teacher spot, but blundering your way out of a murder conviction doesn't make you some hot-shot detective. Get the hell out of my office. Now."

NOTHING QUITE EQUALS a Valentine's Day party for fifth graders. The students were young enough to want a card from everyone, and old enough to care who gave them which cards. It always amazed Diega how much significance the students could read into those innocuous, multi-pack Valentine's cards.

Diega could remember her own childhood and her conflicted feelings around Valentine's Day. She knew what other girls said about their feelings for those boys, but she was also aware that the mild attraction she felt for a few of the males was more friendly than passionate. That heterosexual attraction was a weak eddy compared to the riptide that pulled her to several of the other girls. It was the beginning of a very disorienting time in her life.

After putting away the last of the paper hearts that had decorated the bulletin board for the past several weeks and replacing them with leprechauns and green pots of gold, Diega straightened the science display table and moved on to her desk.

Jim Tolkien threw himself into a student's chair and slid it up beside Diega. "It's been over a week now. The police are never going to figure this out."

Diega did not look up while she sorted student folders into boxes by group. The students' final projects on the Civil War had been presented that day and then heaped upon a table. Although pleased that her students had created diverse ways of presenting the causes and outcomes of the war, she was worried that her words of wisdom regarding organization were not sinking into their consciousness. Sighing at the mound, she continued to ignore Jim's pontification on police incompetence.

Her inattention did not stop him.

"The cops don't think beyond their preconceived ideas. If the wife didn't do it, it must be a family member. If it's not a family member, then it must be a lover or a competitor. Past that, it's got to be random." Jim tapped his foot rapidly against the floor. "No imagination."

Diega labeled the last of the boxes and turned to face her co-worker. "I may regret asking this, but what imaginative theory would you have them examine?"

"Espionage."

"Oh, right. Zeke was stealing top-secret educational secrets from the United States and selling them to the Chinese. Somehow I don't see our educational methods being worth money to anyone else. Some might even say they aren't worth anything at all."

"Right-wing propaganda. The Republicans are the ones who keep trying to tear our system down. If the government would fund education properly—"

Diega cut him off with a wave of her hand. "I've heard it, Jim. Now what is this about Zeke?"

Jim crossed his arms over his chest. "Zeke was seen sneaking in and out of Vista in the early morning and in the evening hours."

"He was meeting with our principal, supposedly on district business."

"That's what the police would like you to think. But what if it was a cover to hide the real reason for his visits? What if you knew there were times he was here when Sally wasn't?"

This comment caught Diega's full attention. "And how would you happen to know that?"

"Someone mentioned it to me."

"Someone just happened to notice who was here when Zeke was and decided to tell you?"

Jim squirmed. "I may have asked some questions." He straightened. "Do you think you're the only one who gets to snoop around and figure things out?"

"My 'snooping,' as you call it, has pretty much been forced upon me. In fact, I seem to remember you were the one who told me to go out and solve Sheila Shelbourne's murder a few years back."

"And I was right, wasn't I?" Jim stomped out the door.

Chapter Eighteen

EAGER TO START her weekend, Diega gathered the boxes of student projects, hauled them outside her door, and turned to lock it. A metallic thud followed by a sharp, loud cracking sound echoed through the hall. After pushing the boxes against the wall, she crept cautiously down the hallway.

The door to Megan Beaker's room was the only open one. Diega peered inside in time to witness Megan kick a wastepaper basket against the wall and hurl the remains of a broken wooden ruler into the corner of the room.

Diega's internal debate about interceding took only seconds. Her better nature won. "Are you okay?"

Megan's head snapped up and the anger that surged through her face quickly dissolved into tears. She slumped into a chair and dropped her head into her hands.

Diega perched on the edge of a desk near the collapsed figure of her sobbing mentee. She reached over and plucked several tissues from the box on the teacher's desk and laid them beside Megan.

Megan grabbed one of the tissues and wiped it haphazardly across her face. "She hates me. No matter what I do. I try so hard and she picks, picks, picks at me."

"She being...?"

"Sally." Megan leaned back and shook her head. "She came in to see me after school to discuss my science lesson. I did all the things you said to do. I hooked this lesson to the previous things we studied, I explained, I demonstrated, I did it all. And she hated it." Tears welled up again. "Then she started screaming at me."

Despite her own run-ins with Sally, Diega was taken aback. "I can't see Sally yelling at you over a lesson."

"Well, she did." Megan blew her nose then looked up at Diega. "After she ripped me apart over my teaching, I was talking with her, trying to, like, be friendly and all and end it on a good note. I complemented her on how hard she worked with Zeke on their proposal and how her husband must be so proud of her." Megan opened her eyes wide. "That's when she blew up. Told me I knew nothing about anything, including teaching, and stormed out of my classroom."

SALLY NELSON WAS still in her office. Diega knocked on her door frame of the principal's office, feeling the need to discuss Sally's reaction to Megan and the lesson.

Sally looked up. Weariness flooded across her face. "How can something so simple go so horribly wrong?"

Sally's first words combined with her furrowed brow made Diega sure the principal was not talking about Megan. "Why don't you start with the simple end and we can work our way forward from there?"

Sally picked up a pencil and jabbed its point into her desk blotter. "The police say there are no other fingerprints except mine on the letter opener. Zeke told the district office that he was coming by Vista to speak to me the morning he died—even though we emphatically did not have an appointment. And now a damned newspaper reporter calls and tells me that Zeke was hitting up companies for payback and telling them that part of the money was going to me." The pencil point snapped. "I expect Detective Theophilus and a pair of handcuffs any second." Sally looked up at Diega. "If that happens, will you please call my husband? And Erin?"

"Don't you want me to call a lawyer, too?"

"No." Sally gave a rueful laugh. "I keep thinking that I don't need a lawyer because I didn't do it. Innocent people don't go to jail in this country." She sank back in her chair and closed her eyes. Shaking herself, she sat up straight. "It's ironic that the one thing I was doing to keep my job in this district is going to be the thing that gets me fired, or worse."

Sally picked up an engraved paperweight and studied it as if it were a crystal ball with all the answers of the world encased in it. "The staff at my last job in Fullerton gave this to me. The school was in a mostly Hispanic neighborhood, high dropout rate, high truancy, seventy-percent limited English speakers. I created student cohorts within classrooms, teacher cohorts within and between grades, and parent cohorts by block. We agonized over every aspect of the school day from curriculum to recess to before- and after-school activities. I visited students at their homes. Our staff started attending the students' sporting events and church performances." She handed the paperweight to Diega. "Attendance increased, tardiness decreased, and we raised test scores by twenty-three percent in a little over two years."

Diega read the inscription on the paperweight: *To Sally Nelson, Our Cheerleader and Taskmaster. Thanks for Making Us Proud of Ourselves.*

Sally went on to explain that when she was hired, the superintendent assigned her to work with Zeke Chambers and write a grant to start such a program in one of the lowest-performing schools in Glendale. The superintendent asked to keep the project under wraps until he could present it to the School Board.

"Zeke was not the best partner for this. He argued with me more than he helped. He kept wanting to outsource curriculum and activities that were integral to the project." She shook her head. "Here I was trying to get used to Vista, and on top of that I had to squeeze in time to write the grant with Zeke. My family didn't know what I looked like anymore. Then Erin took off to Europe and Patrick was left totally alone." She stopped and a pained expression filled her eyes.

"Were you having an affair with Zeke?"

Sally rocked back in her chair. Her eyes narrowed. "How dare you!"

Diega held up her hand. "I dare because that is exactly what everyone is saying." Diega waited until she thought Sally was listening to her again. "You've got to realize that the teachers are all gossiping about the hours you and Zeke were locked together. Even his wife suspected there was something going on."

Sally slapped her desktop and stood. Her head reared back and she stared down at Diega. "Zeke Chambers was a loathsome parasite without an original thought in his head. I hated working with that bastard. I tried to get out of the assignment because I knew if I had to spend any more time with that creep I'd — "

Diega raised an eyebrow. "Kill him?"

A knock on the doorframe interrupted. Detective Theophilus and two officers stood in the doorway. He nodded at Diega, but his eyes were focused on Sally.

"Mrs. Nelson, I am placing you under arrest for the attempted murder of Luis Hernandez."

"LUIS, I AM so glad to see you." Diega reached over tubes and around machines in order to squeeze the custodian's hand as he lay in the bed.

Once the police had handcuffed Sally and escorted her out, Theophilus had told Diega that Luis was awake and allowed limited visitation. After calling Sally's husband and speaking briefly with Erin, who promised to call an attorney, Diega drove over to Glendale Mercy Hospital. She had had to show her ID and be cleared by the officer who guarded the hospital room before being admitted.

"Not as happy as I am to see you, Diega." Luis tried to smile, but it betrayed the weakness of his body. "I thank you for my life. My family is lighting candles for you in church each morning."

"I'll take all the help I can get," Diega said, glossing over the fact that she had not been inside a church in over a decade. She asked about his progress and about his family.

"The doctors decided I was awake enough this morning to talk with the police. If I keep making progress like this, I will be getting out of here in a few days," Luis said. "I sent my daughter back to school. I told her she needed to study more than I needed her to watch my every breath. My wife does a good enough job of that."

"Do you have any idea who did this to you?"

"I do not know. The police told me they think it was Mrs. Nelson, but I can't believe that. She is a good person. A kind person." Luis shook his head slowly. "That morning I was getting my mop and pail ready for the lunchroom. I don't have enough time to set it up once the children start coming, so I always set up before 7:00 when I open the doors for the teachers. I don't remember hearing anything. Only the pain." He closed his eyes and grimaced.

"What time did you get to work?"

"The usual. 6:00."

"Were any of the teachers there? Or any parents?"

"I'm the only one there that early. Well, sometimes Mrs. Nelson comes in around 6:30. But she wasn't there that morning. I'm sure. There were no cars in the parking lot and I didn't hear anyone come in."

"Were the outside doors locked?"

"Always. I always make sure I relock the side door when I come in. The teachers all have the key for that door anyway. I don't unlock the front door until 7:30 when Mrs. Kirk comes in."

Diega was surprised that Mrs. Kirk, the new school secretary, did not have her own key, but she was not sure following that particular thread would lead anywhere. She shifted her focus. "I'm sure the police have asked you already, but do you know why someone wanted to hurt you?"

Again he shook his head.

"Did you ever notice Zeke Chambers around?"

"Yes. Of course. He came many mornings to work with Mrs. Nelson."

"Was he always near Sally's office? Did you ever see him in other parts of the school?"

"He was always in the office, except for the morning he was killed."

"Where was he then?"

"In the hallway outside of your classroom. I thought he might have a meeting with you because he was leaning against the wall beside your room and he kept checking his watch. He was there when I finished sweeping the hallway, which is a lot earlier than he usually was when he met Mrs. Nelson."

"What time was that?"

Luis closed his eyes briefly. Diega could not tell if he was in thought or in pain. But he answered, "About 6:20."

"Did you see who he met?"

"No. I left to clean the front office."

Diega chewed her lower lip. She felt sure there was something else to get, but was unsure of what question would elicit the information.

Luis did the work for her. "You understand I told the police about Mr. Chambers. They asked me if I saw anyone else and I said no. But I was thinking about the people who work at school, not other people."

Diega nodded encouragingly.

"I did see someone else that morning. Not a teacher. Mrs. Nelson's husband."

"Patrick?" Diega tried to weave this new piece of information into the fabric of that morning. "Was he in Sally's office?"

"No. He was knocking on the front door. When I opened it, he asked if I had seen his wife. When I told him no, he walked down the hall to the side door."

"Did he say why he was looking for his wife?"

"No. But it must not have been good news."

"Why?"

"He looked very angry."

Chapter Nineteen

DIEGA DROVE STRAIGHT to the Nelson's house. She didn't know if they would be there or at the police station, but she decided the element of surprise might be a good tactic.

Erin answered her knock. "Diega. Has something else happened? Have you heard from Marsha?"

"Nothing like that. I'm sure Marsha will call you as soon as they finish processing your mom." Diega realized that was not the most reassuring thing she might have said, but Erin seemed to take it well. "I actually wanted to talk with you and your dad."

Erin invited Diega inside. "Thanks again for calling about Mom. I don't know when we would have heard otherwise."

The living room was large and opened onto the dining room and kitchen. Cool, pastel colors graced the walls, which were covered in photographs and paintings. Diega thought the décor complemented the mid-century modern house. Before she could get more than an impression of the surroundings, a worried-looking Patrick Nelson came into the room, hand extended. "Thank you for recommending a lawyer. I don't know what we would have done. Have you heard anything?"

Diega shook his hand. "Marsha will call you when she knows about bail or anything else. She's a good lawyer." Diega hated admitting anything good about her former rival, but she knew it was true. "I was wondering if I could talk with you about the day of Zeke Chambers's murder."

Wariness grew in Patrick's eyes. "Why would you want to talk to me about that?"

"I just came from visiting Luis Hernandez. You should know he's awake and talking."

Patrick invited her to take a seat. She sank into a puffy armchair while Patrick and his daughter sat side by side on the couch.

Patrick cleared his throat. "Now what is this about Mr. Hernandez?"

"He mentioned that on the day that Zeke died you were at school early in the morning and that you were very angry."

"Was I?"

Diega bluffed. "You were looking for your wife and Zeke. You knew about their affair and you were going to put a stop to it."

"Dad! You didn't!" Erin's anguished cry seemed to do more than Diega's accusation to spur Patrick into speech.

"Honey, it wasn't like that at all."

Erin shifted to stare at him. "But you were there? At school?" Before he could respond she turned to Diega. "He didn't kill Zeke.

No matter what anyone saw."

Diega ignored Erin and, instead, addressed Patrick. "If you truly want to help your wife, the truth needs to come out."

Patrick rubbed his face with both hands, his whiskers creating a rasping noise. When he finally spoke, he looked at his daughter, not Diega. "I was at Vista that morning and I was looking for your mom. I wasn't really looking for Zeke, but I did run into him on my way out." He reached over to grab Erin's hand before she could speak. "When I saw him I... We argued. He looked kind of edgy and suggested we discuss this in a more private place. He opened a classroom and we went inside."

Patrick sat forward and leaned his arms on his knees. "We argued some more. He made a crack about your mom and I lost it."

"Dad, stop," Erin said, grabbing his arm. "Don't say anything else."

Patrick enveloped Erin's hand with his. "No, honey. Diega's right. I should have told the police this. I want to get it out." This time he looked at Diega. "When Zeke made his comment, I clobbered him. I think I must have broken his nose. I certainly bruised my knuckles." He raised his right hand and stared at his balled up fist. After a deep breath, he continued his story. "He fell back against the counter then he stood up. He was dripping blood."

Diega prodded. "Then what happened?"

"I left. I slammed the door and stormed out to my truck and drove away. I almost hit the car in front of me I was so angry." Patrick looked back at his daughter. "He was alive when I left. Pissed, bleeding, but alive. You've got to believe me."

Erin released his hands in order to wrap her arms around him.

Diega broke into the family moment. "Why don't you start from the beginning of that morning?"

Patrick kissed Erin on the forehead, then sat up straight. "Sally left early. Said she had a meeting. I asked if she was meeting Zeke, but she said no. I didn't believe her." He folded his hands together, slowly tightening and releasing his fingers as he spoke. "I paced around for a few minutes, arguing with myself. But I couldn't stand it anymore. I had to know. So I got into my truck and headed to Vista. I parked around the side of the building so Sally wouldn't notice my car. I tried a side door, but it was locked. I walked around to the front. Sally's car wasn't there. That confused me."

Diega asked, "Was there a car parked in front of yours?"

Patrick squinted at her as if he had forgotten she was there. "A black Jaguar. Why?"

"Never mind. So you went around to the front of the school?"

"Yeah. I looked through the window but I couldn't see into Sally's office. So, I figured, what the hell, the element of surprise is gone anyhow, so I pounded on the door. The custodian let me in."

"You said Zeke opened a classroom. Which classroom was it and how did he open it?"

"It was on the side wing of the building. Second classroom on the right. He opened it with a key."

Diega asked, "Was the key on a keychain or was it separate?"

"It was separate. He pulled it out of his pocket."

"Are you sure it was the second, not the third room?"

Patrick nodded.

Erin looked puzzled. She addressed Diega. "Isn't that your classroom? But that isn't where Zeke was murdered."

"No, but it's starting to explain some things." Diega turned her attention back to Patrick. "Did you tell Sally any of this?"

He nodded. "The detective came to the house last Sunday asking Sally a lot of questions. After he left, I told her the whole story."

"Sunday?" Erin's eyes went wide. She grabbed her dad's hand.

Diega could tell that the same thought had occurred to her: Luis was attacked the very next day.

SATURDAY MORNING, THE light bloomed over the hills surrounding Burbank, but it brought no accompanying illumination for Diega's beleaguered brain. She decided to switch to a jogging route along Clark Avenue as a way to push her thoughts into new pathways.

A shout brought Diega's attention back to her jog. She waved in return to Jack. He, of iridescent green shorts, was on the opposite side of the street and had his two massive German Shepherds running with him, so Diega did not stop to chat.

Few cars travelled this road at 5:30 in the morning and Diega was appreciative of the quiet. She passed Mort's Meat Mart and decided to keep going to Buena Vista. At the corner of Clark and Buena Vista, she turned left, briefly fantasizing about continuing her run to Olive, over the hill on Barham Boulevard, and on into Hollywood, far away from all the craziness that surrounded her. Instead, she jogged to Verdugo and turned left again back toward home. On her right, before she turned the corner, she caught sight of the old one-story beige, stucco building that housed the Buena Vista Branch Public Library. The vision caused a thought to waft through her brain, but it was too vague to hold. With a mental shrug she trotted homeward.

To her surprise, her neighbor, Mrs. Holmes, was in her yard. Diega called a greeting and Mrs. Holmes waved her cane in return.

"I was picking up the *Times* and I finally remembered," Mrs. Holmes said, now leaning on her stick. "It's about that man who was killed at your school."

"Zeke Chambers? What about him?" Diega wiped her forehead with her wrist sweatband.

"I told you that young man looked familiar, but it wasn't until I saw today's front page that I recalled where I saw him before." She thrust the paper at Diega.

Diega took it and saw the below-the-fold story of a large audit of the Glendale district's funds. A picture of a smiling Zeke Chambers graced the side of the article.

Mrs. Holmes pointed with her cane. "He was at the Burbank Board of Education meeting last year. Talking about some cockamamie scheme that Glendale had come up with that he thought we should try." Mrs. Holmes sniffed. "That Glendale thinks it can tell us what to do just because we're smaller. It wants to push its big city ways on us." Now she shook her cane at Diega. "Don't you come home with that kind of nonsense in your head."

"I wouldn't dream of it," Diega said, although she was not exactly sure what she had sworn not to take under consideration. "Did the school board accept Zeke's suggestions?"

"They did not. Sent him off with a flea in his ear, I will tell you. As well they should."

After ascertaining that May of the previous year was the approximate month of Zeke's appearance, Diega grabbed her own paper from her front lawn and headed into the house and the shower. As she scrubbed she realized what had niggled at her brain concerning the library. She knew both Burbank and Glendale telecasted their school board and city council meetings. She thought she might view a couple of Zeke's presentation to the Glendale Board of Education and see if she could figure out what other projects he had been pushing. Now, thanks to Mrs. Holmes, she decided she would extend her search to the Burbank school board as well.

Although the Burbank Leader was not exactly the place to find in-depth reporting, Diega considered the twice-weekly local paper to be a reasonably accurate source of events around the town. Saturday's lead article concerned the Glendale and Burbank Boards of Education uniting to undertake an investigation into all outsourced projects including charter schools. Her opinion of the newspaper skyrocketed when she realized that the reporter had actually gone beyond the official news release and had done some background research.

The article included the interesting fact that Zeke Chambers had taken out a license to do business as Education Edge, a charter school company.

Diega's mind stirred. She remembered Gwen mentioning Education Edge as a rival who was trying to move in on the Glendale schools.

The article continued with a description of the pitch that Education Edge was giving in a brochure it had produced. It proclaimed a new approach to education using multi-level classrooms, which allowed for older students to tutor younger students, reinforcing learning and social connections. It also included a mandate of parent involvement in the school and teacher community.

Diega reread the description of the Education Edge brochure. She laid the paper on the table and leaned back in her chair. She wondered if

Sally Nelson would have access to this article. If so, Sally could not help but notice all her groundbreaking ideas presented as the basis for Zeke's enterprise. Diega bet that if Sally knew what Zeke had done, she would surely kill him. If she had not already done so.

Diega also realized that Jim Tolkien was right. In a way, Zeke was engaged in espionage, not for the Chinese, but rather for his own profit. He had picked the brains of Sally Nelson and probably every company he did business with to create this new enterprise of his.

Ironically, Diega rather approved of the meld he had developed. This was the one approach that could indeed hit the million-dollar jackpot of improving the results for lower-income students. All Zeke would have had to do was to sell the idea that this type of alternative education was necessary in Glendale.

The plot of an old movie suddenly popped into Diega's head: Robert Preston as the shyster Harold Hill in the "Music Man." How did he sell the need for a boy's band in River City, Iowa? By creating trouble using an otherwise benign pool table.

A sinking feeling hit Diega as she wondered if she was the pool table that Zeke had used for access to Glendale. If the information he leaked her caused problems for the district, that might make the educational system look broken. And if those troubles were widely known in the community, perhaps the people would go looking for Professor Harold Hill, in the form of Zeke Chambers, for a fix.

BY THE TIME the library opened at ten o'clock, Diega was pacing in front of the wide front steps that led to an old, double-wide wooden door. There was talk of building a new Buena Vista Library, but Diega enjoyed the homey feel of this vintage structure and hoped the city would come up with other projects to occupy its attention and money.

Built-in bookcases lit by low-hanging fluorescent lights formed the walls of the building. Wide, arched doorways separated the rooms. Free-standing bookcases and magazine racks crowded the middle of the rooms. Eight-foot wooden tables with sturdy wooden chairs filled the rest of the floor space. Diega picked her way between these to reach the desk of the reference librarian. Diega asked about recorded meetings of the Burbank Board of Education. The dark-haired woman quietly directed her to a back shelf with neatly labeled plastic cases. Inside were videotapes of the meetings. She found May of the previous year and plucked March through July, too, just to be sure.

Back home, she slid the May meeting tape into her video player and settled into the couch. Both cats immediately joined her for an unusual daytime snuggle. They took turns walking across Diega's lap before deciding to plop on either side of her.

After fast-forwarding through most of it, she determined that Zeke was not present that month. It took her three tries before hitting upon the right meeting.

It was a jolt for Diega to see Zeke Chambers — combed-back brown hair, jutting chin, silver-rimmed glasses, and crinkly smile — alive and addressing the Board. She rewound and listened carefully, starting with the introduction.

Presented as an assistant to the superintendent of Glendale, Zeke made no mention of being there as a private citizen. But his speech was clearly a sales job for an educational software company that Glendale did not even use. Diega's disgust grew with every minute of his appearance.

When the question-and-answer period ended and Zeke was leaving the podium, Diega started to fast-forward through the rest. The camera, however, followed Zeke back to his seat. There a familiar face caught Diega's eye. She stopped the video, then reversed it. Then she froze the picture.

There, smiling happily up at Zeke Chambers, was Diega's teaching neighbor and occupant of the room where Zeke was murdered, Rita Morgan.

Chapter Twenty

THE TELEPHONE INTERRUPTED Diega's contemplation of Rita's possible involvement with Zeke. Surprise replaced reflection as she realized the voice on the phone belonged to her principal's husband, Patrick Nelson.

"Can you come over and talk some sense into Erin? She won't talk to me. She won't talk to Marsha. Sally's still in jail, so she can't talk to her."

"What's the problem?"

"Erin is telling us that she killed Zeke."

Stunned, Diega listened as Patrick outlined how Erin had burst into the police station and demanded to see the detective in charge of the case. "I went to the station to tell them about my fight with Zeke. Erin must have followed. As soon as that detective released me, Erin insisted on talking with him. She was actually arguing with him, ordering him to arrest her." His voice sounded weary. "They didn't believe her. They obviously thought she was making it all up to save Sally." He paused. "Honestly, I don't know if she was doing it for her mom or for me, but I think she's made it worse for both of us."

A KOI POND fed by a natural stone waterfall occupied the far left corner of the Nelson's backyard. Erin was crouched beside the water throwing little pellets to the fish. She rose as Diega walked toward her. Her eyes were wary and Diega sensed a warning in them. It was a warning Diega ignored.

"What in the hell were you thinking?" Diega reached out and grabbed Erin's shoulders. She was tempted to shake her, but refrained.

Erin wrenched away. "My parents had nothing to do with any of this. I've caused them enough grief. They don't need this, too."

Diega threw her arms in the air. "You just think you've caused them grief. What do you think it would do to them to have you hauled away on murder charges?"

Erin crossed her arms and turned away.

Diega sank onto a cement bench angled beside the pond. She gripped her hands together firmly. Forcing her voice into a reasonable tone, she said, "Confessing to something you didn't do is not going to help them in the long run. Besides, the police will figure out a bogus admission fairly easily."

Arms still crossed, Erin turned to face Diega. "What makes you think it's bogus? I knew my parents' marriage was in trouble. My dad admitted to me that he thought Mom was interested in someone else.

Why wouldn't I track down her lover and kill him?"

"How did you know who he was and where he was going to be that morning?"

"That doesn't matter. I followed my dad and heard him argue with Zeke. When Dad ran out of the room, I went in. I picked up the scissors and stabbed him."

Diega pushed herself out off the bench and stood in front of Erin. "That account is wrong on so many levels. The police will never believe it."

"I'll make them believe it."

"And then what? You think it'll all fall apart at the trial and the police will magically decide to close the investigation?"

"It doesn't matter." Erin crossed her arms more tightly. "I'll be dead before then."

Diega opened her mouth to tell Erin that that was a sick joke, but the look on Erin's face stopped her. She took a breath instead. "Before I say anything, maybe you'd better explain that little remark."

Erin unwrapped her arms and waved Diega back onto the bench. Erin sat next to Diega. She rubbed the back of her neck before hunching over and clasping her hands together. "Two years ago I had breast cancer. I had a lumpectomy, chemo, and radiation." She rubbed the bridge of her nose with her thumbs. "Katie left me. Couldn't take the ups and downs of the treatment. Then there were my parents — hovering, anxious, wanting to help, and being helpless. It was emotionally and physically exhausting."

Erin paused, but Diega remained silent, sensing there was more to the story.

Erin shuddered as if to shake off the memories. "So when I survived the ordeal and got some energy back, I decided that I was going to live life and not wait until I was older to have some adventures. Despite Mom's protests, I took a leave from my job and zoomed off for Europe as soon as I was cleared to fly." Erin shifted. "The chemo had taken its toll. I had neuropathy in my fingers and toes. Despite that, I went mountain climbing, skiing, and rappelling. All the time I pushed aside the thought of check-ups and clearances, the whole medical thing." She looked over at Diega. "But my doctor contacted me and basically ordered me to go to a clinic she knew in Zurich. Rather than giving me the once-over, they gave me a complete check-up including a mammogram and ultrasound." Erin leaned back, crossing her arms over her chest. "They found another mass in my breast. So I flew home. I didn't tell my folks I was coming because I wanted to have my doctors do their own tests." She smiled a smile that held no humor. "Remember the day you rescued me from the bar? That's the day my doctor called and confirmed the results. It's cancer. Again. And it's spread."

WHEN DIEGA RETURNED from the Nelson's house, she felt a need to clean. She gathered up her dirty clothes and sorted them into piles by weight and color. The oft-repeated task of washing clothes freed her mind to wander. Where it wandered, however, was not to her liking. Despite her best intentions, her thoughts jumped immediately back to Erin. Breast cancer. Erin with breast cancer and all that entailed. Diega's stomach tightened and her breathing became shallow.

Breast cancer had never before invaded Diega's life. The news stories and medical breakthroughs had washed over her, not having anywhere near the impact that the AIDS epidemic had. That disease had baptized Diega into the realm of illness and helplessness as she watched three of her best male friends die slowly and horribly in the last decade.

Now the thought of lovely, lively, young Erin Nelson stricken with a recurrence of what could be a deadly disease overwhelmed Diega. Forcefully, she yanked her thoughts from the possibly dying to the already dead. On one level it appalled her that thinking about Zeke was easier than dwelling on Erin's fate. But she acknowledged the reality and distracted herself with a turn down the road of murderous intent.

As she was adding bleach into the dispenser for the white load, she almost spilled some on her jeans. The drops spraying out from the dispenser made the blood spatter across Zeke's punctured back swim into focus. Most people were wearing long-sleeved shirts this time of year, so wouldn't the person who stabbed him have blood on his cuffs if not other parts of his clothes? If so, wouldn't other people notice a blood splattered shirt?

Diega slammed the washing machine's door shut, yanked the knob to start the water, and forced herself to concentrate on Zeke's murder.

Despite the fact that Tully and Gina were coming to dinner that night, Diega wasn't ready to deal with dinner preparations. Instead she wandered into the kitchen where she fixed a cup of Earl Grey tea. Armed with the warm stimulant, she settled on the couch. Start from the beginning, she commanded herself. The scene of the crime.

There was blood in her room even though Zeke's body was next door. If the blood in her room was Zeke's, could he have been wounded in her room and then staggered down the hall to collapse and die in Rita's? If so, why would he have done so? It's not like he could get help in another room.

What, she thought, if the blood in her room was from the weapon used to kill Zeke? Maybe the murderer stabbed Zeke in Rita's room and then came next door and laid the bloody scissors on the floor. And then returned to Rita's room to plunge them back into Zeke again? That made even less sense.

Needing more caffeine, she refilled the pot and turned on the burner once again. As she toiled, the mystery of why Zeke bled in one place and died in another slid to the back of her brain. The larger question of why he was killed at Vista Elementary School took its place.

Who would know Zeke would be there that morning? People at the district office? Sally? Zeke's wife? His son? It did not seem likely that Carl and his ilk would know Zeke was there. Unless, Diega thought, Zeke was using the school as a safe meeting spot. Maybe a spot for a money drop-off.

Her deliberations leapt to Zeke's pursuit of money. If he had enough money to buy that house and a vacation home in Morro Bay, send his kids to a private school, and put on the parties that his wife seemed to love so much, why did he need more? What had happened to increase his expenses so much that he would branch out into illegal endeavors?

Or were illegal activities how he made his money in the first place?

Zeke, she thought, may well turn out to be a slime ball. But he couldn't have sole claim to the title. There were ten million other guys just as dirty who still manage to walk the planet. What had he done that was so horrific as to enrage someone to the point that they shish-kabobbed him?

The last mental comparison was inaccurate, but perhaps subconsciously motivated, Diega realized, since she knew her planned menu for the evening included beef kabobs.

The buzzing of the washer brought Diega back to her living room and the reality that guests would be arriving in a couple of hours.

After finishing the laundry, Diega gave the barbeque grill a light coat of oil before clicking the ignition button and turning on the gas. A pop signaled the emergence of flames. She closed the top of the barbeque to preheat, then she laid out the tongs and spatula on the side table. Finally, she checked the spray bottle to make sure it was full of water. Even though she knew she was not supposed to use it on a gas fire, and she never had used it, she felt more secure knowing it was nearby. Satisfied, she returned to the kitchen to finish preparing the main dish and vegetables.

Tully and Gina arrived at 6:30 exactly. Gina, with her tall, sleek, dark, Mediterranean looks, blended nicely with the even taller and more rounded Tully. Diega liked the older woman, although she had difficulty understanding how Gina tolerated Tully's dalliances. Giving only a fleeting thought to her own one indiscretion and its aftermath, Diega shrugged internally and poured some wine.

Gina accepted the glass of deep red wine and followed Diega out to the deck. She watched as Diega adjusted the flames and flipped the tinfoil-wrapped vegetable mix. Diega could feel Gina's dark eyes studying her back. Diega glanced over her shoulder and raised an eyebrow.

Gina swirled the red wine in her glass. "I got an interesting call from a Glendale PD detective."

Diega turned her attention back to the grill and adjusted the vegetable packet.

"Seems this Detective Theophilus thought I could be some sort of character witness for you."

Diega felt heat flood her face and knew it was not from the flames. She looked over her shoulder and said sheepishly, "I guess I invoked your name as a higher power. I needed him to realize I wasn't some crank sending him off on a snipe hunt."

"And you thought I'd vouch for you? With your record of butting in on murder investigations?"

"I don't butt in!"

"That's right," Tully said as she flopped into a patio chair beside Gina. "She doesn't back into them. She walks in face-first."

Diega squirted Tully with the water bottle.

Gina chuckled and handed Tully her napkin. She turned back to Diega. "So what snipe are you trying to send this Theophilus guy off after?"

Diega reported on the affair, interrupted frequently by Tully's enthusiastic, if slightly colorful, version of events. She slid the beef kabobs onto the grill as she ended with, "Now Erin has complicated matters by telling the police that she murdered Zeke."

The thunk of wine glasses hitting the table caused Diega to turn around. Gina and Tully both stared at her.

"She didn't. She's hoping it will divert suspicion from either of her parents."

"That's still a plum-fool thing to do," Tully said, retrieving her glass. "What if they had believed her?"

"She doesn't think it will matter." Diega explained about the recurrence of Erin's cancer.

"Oh my God." Gina's eyes held pain. "My aunt died from breast cancer last year. That poor girl. I can't even imagine what she must be going through."

Tully said, "We have to call Jenny. With all her hospital contacts, she'd know the top cancer doctors. Or she'd know who to ask."

"It couldn't hurt." Diega turned back to the kabobs. She could not look at her friends as she delivered the last bit of news. "A second opinion might give her some new options. Frankly, the ones she laid out did not sound appealing. More like a choice between a slow death with a lot of pain or a prolonged one with massive surgery. Neither mentioned much chance of a cure, let alone many years of survival."

"Shit." Gina summation matched Diega's opinion exactly.

"This totally sucks." Tully took a long swallow of wine before adding, "Dee, buddy, you're loading your wagon kinda high. Sure you want to add a wounded kitten onto your other extracurricular activities?

"I don't think you could ever describe Erin as a wounded kitten. A wounded tiger, maybe, but a kitten, never."

"Then you'd better watch yourself, kiddo. A wounded tiger is very dangerous to be around."

Gina studied the remnants of her wine. "Do I detect a personal interest in this matter?"

"Of course it's personal," Diega said, reverting to the original discussion. "I found Zeke's body. It's my school, and my classroom, and my principal."

Gina swirled the last bit of wine and then downed it. "Your principal wasn't the one I was referring to."

Diega ignored the comment and refilled Gina's glass. "Do you investigate the bank records of victims?"

Gina twitched an eyebrow. "Do I sense a change of topic?" She shook her head. "I look into the financial records, the family situation, the work relationships, the relationship history. I look under any rock I can, especially when there are no readily apparent leads."

"Do banks cooperate with the police?"

"Not without a court order, so we go to the banks last. Why?"

"I'm wondering if the police might have checked to see if Zeke had unusual amounts of money going in or out of his account. If he's heavy into gambling, he might have sudden drops in his bank accounts."

"Or gains if he's been lucky," Tully said. "Of course the upswings in his monetary funds could also be due to silver crossing his palm in exchange for his services."

Gina took a deep breath. She laid her hand firmly on Tully's shoulder. "Diega, I somewhat trust you not to go hog-wild on this. I have no such faith in your friend here," she said, shaking Tully. She looked at Diega. "If you have these questions, you might want to call Theophilus and tell him. I wouldn't do the personal phone calls too often, though. Your detective friend seemed like he has a more than passing interest in you—and not as a suspect."

Chapter Twenty-one

RESTLESS AFTER THE departure of Tully and Gina, Diega knew it was pointless to try to sleep. Instead she fired up her desktop computer and set to work. She had taken an adult education class about the internet and had learned to use the new search engines that helped locate information. She started with the Ask Jeeves site and entered Zeke's name. He did not have a personal website, but, then, Diega couldn't think of anyone she knew who did. Nor did Education Edge turn up on the search results. But Zeke's name appeared multiple times in the one year of Board of Education minutes the GUSD had posted. Diega started down the list of documents.

Lloyd's information on Zeke's involvement in the vetting of Brighter Days seemed accurate. Zeke was listed as the liaison officer for the district and was mentioned in the Board of Education minutes as having taken part in the presentation to the Board when the project was voted upon.

Beyond that, Zeke's name was mentioned in connection with five more vendors asking for contracts to provide everything from educational services to software and computers to the district. Diega could not decide if Zeke endorsed everything that came his way or if the district only listed the ones that he brought forward for approval. In either case, all but one of Zeke's projects won the support of the Board. Diega added up a total of $3.5 million in contracts in the last year that the district had awarded based, at least in part, on Zeke's backing.

Diega leaned back in her chair, an action BB took as a signal that lap time had arrived. She slithered off the desk and collapsed on Diega's lap. The vibration of her purrs massaged Diega's legs. Diega absently petted BB's ebony fur while staring at the list on her computer screen.

If Zeke picked up a kickback from these companies, he could have seen three hundred thousand dollars added to his bank account. That might make the police take notice. Unless Zeke somehow had a hidden account. Diega was fuzzy on the ins and outs of creating an account under a different name. Her bank always asked for her ID when she withdrew money. Maybe it was different if you put the money in stocks or precious metal? She decided Tully might be the one to ask.

SUNDAY MORNING BROUGHT a pounding on Diega's front door. Tully waved as Diega peered through the peephole. Diega shook off drowsiness and opened the door to her friend.

Tully bounded into the room. "I'm dragging your pretty derriere out of the house for breakfast."

"What roused you at this hour?"

"I have news. Mini-mustache boy has disappeared."

"You mean Zeke's son?"

"Yep. According to Gina, his mom filed a missing persons report with Glendale PD yesterday and they've passed along the info to all the surrounding departments."

Diega curled herself onto one corner of the couch while Tully threw herself onto the other side. She considered what she knew about Wayne. "Is his Harley missing, too?"

"Yep. But no one's reported it on the road or any of the usual motel hot spots."

"They may want to check the card club parking lots as well." Diega thought of Wayne's run-in with black-clad Carl at the poker club. Then she thought of what Carl had done to Harrison. "If Carl got him, they may be fishing his body out of a lake somewhere."

"I mentioned that to Gina. She said the police have no cause, so far, to have any kind of surveillance on our favorite moneylender. But she also pointed out that there's no reason to think that Carl is after Wayne." Tully let out a long breath. "The police don't know if something happened to make Wayne disappear or if he's done it on his own. There's really no reason to think he's been kidnapped — no ransom note, no threatening phone calls."

"I don't think Carl would send any love letters. A beaten body seems to work well for him. But Gina's right. Why would Carl bother with Wayne?" Diega felt a caffeine craving coming on. "Any thoughts as to why Wayne would want to skip town on his own?"

"Other than the fact that he seems to hate his mother?"

"If every kid who hated his mother ran away from home, damn few households would include children."

"True. But this isn't my only reason for coming by. I need some ocean time and I wanted my best buddy to share it with me." Tully reached over and slapped Diega's knee. "So get yourself dressed and let's go for a drive."

"If coffee is included, it's a deal. I can fill you in on my ideas along the way."

In the car, Diega explained her findings of the night before.

"Now what made you think I'd be an expert on money laundering?" Tully said after Diega had explained her idea. "Besides, don't you think the police might check on that angle?"

"That's only if the police think Zeke was skimming money. It's not a sure thing that they've heard the rumors."

"Want me to ask Gina?"

"No. Glendale's not her jurisdiction and I'm not really sure Zeke did any of this. I really shouldn't be thinking about this at all, but I can't seem to stop."

"Dee, if you weren't thinking about this, I'd be taking your temperature. However, I need to switch the focus for a minute. I think I've come up with a great celebration for Jenny and Felicia."

Tully explained that she had checked into renting the Equestrian Center on the border of Burbank and Glendale for a Texas barbeque. She had some friends who would put on a rodeo demonstration and a band that would play country-western music for dancing. The only thing she was lacking was a chuck-wagon cook.

Diega was glad to be able to add something to the plans. "The husband of one of the teachers at school runs a barbeque place. Let me talk with him about a possible menu and what he'd charge."

"Good deal." Tully released one hand from the Jeep's steering wheel and snapped her fingers. "I just thought of someone I could ask about bank accounts, legal and otherwise." She grinned at Diega. "Zeke's murderer doesn't know it yet, but he's about to have the Cagney and Lacey of the nineties on his tail."

"Before we pin badges on our chests, let me run another idea by you." Diega gripped the armrest as the car sailed over a bump on the freeway. She briefly wondered where all the gasoline tax monies were being spent before focusing once again on her main thread. "What's the first thing you'd do if somebody broke your nose?"

"Are you presuming I'd be so crude as to get into a fist fight with someone? Please."

"Let's say your nose is broken and you're bleeding all over the place. What would you do?"

"Grab a towel and get some ice."

"Exactly. Lacking ice, you'd go for water," Diega said. "You'd probably go over to the sink, get some paper towels, and maybe turn on the water to wash off the blood."

"I presume this is a veiled reference to the Zeke and Patrick fight, right?"

When Diega nodded, Tully continued, "So you think after Zeke got clobbered, he walked over to your sink?"

"No."

Tully flicked an eyebrow.

Diega explained. "I think that would be the normal thing to do. But there were no drops of blood leading to the sink. There was only that one puddle by the science table."

"Maybe he had a handkerchief or something to stop the flow."

"Maybe. But, if so, he sure wasn't holding it when he was killed. Or, at least, I didn't see one."

Tully frowned at Diega. "You're talking like you've got the doggies all rounded up."

"Not all, but some of them." Diega leaned forward and ticked off her fingers. "One, Zeke was waiting for someone. Two, he had a master key. Three, he chose my room probably because it was not the room he was going to meet someone in. Four, he might have gotten paper towels from my sink, but he sure didn't get any water because the pipes were broken. Fifth, unless he levitated, there was no way for him to get to the sink without leaving a trail of blood."

"A gory Hansel and Gretel," Tully said. "So is that when he hightailed it to your neighbor's room?"

Diega shook her head. "He couldn't go anywhere without leaving his bloody breadcrumbs and there were none in the hallway."

Understanding flooded Tully's face. "So you think someone helped him."

"You got it. The mysterious person he was meeting. Think about it. Patrick Nelson sure didn't stick around to tend to Zeke's wounds. Mr. X must have grabbed some towels and given them to Zeke. Maybe they tried the sink and found it broken. It would make sense to go to another classroom and clean Zeke up."

Tully joined in. "Being in pain and all, Zeke would hand his good buddy his key to unlock the other door."

"Exactly. I bet you a buck that the police found bloody paper towels in Rita's room."

Tully chewed over the conjectures. "That would mean the person our Zeke boy was meeting ended up killed him."

"That's my guess."

Tully turned off the freeway and onto Venice Boulevard heading west, toward the beach. "I hate to pour liquid sunshine on your protest march, but there are two little pieces that your version doesn't cover. One, why did someone who wants to kill Zeke care so much about him that he helps care for Zeke's bloody nose? And two, why did your mysterious stranger go after the school custodian?"

The car was silent except for the crunch of tires on the road.

Tully paid the five dollars and pulled into the beach parking lot. She turned in her seat and faced her passenger. "Now, Dee, I know it would break your heart to think that somebody lied to you, but let's pretend that Sally's hubby really did kill Zeke. That gives him or his wife the perfect motive for wanting your custodian friend out of the way. This Patrick guy must have realized the custodian hadn't told the police yet about seeing him, so maybe he decided to take care of that little loose end before the custodian spilled the guacamole. Or maybe his wife decided to cover for him."

"Maybe. But the psychology is all wrong for Patrick being the murderer."

Tully groaned. "If you are going to lecture me about criminal minds, I'm going to have to have a mimosa with breakfast."

Diega ignored her protest. "If Patrick's mad enough to kill Zeke, then after punching Zeke, he'd strangle him or something equally gruesome. I somehow don't see Patrick handing Zeke a paper towel, escorting him into another room, and then finding some scissors to stab him with. It makes no sense. So if Patrick didn't do it, someone else may have the same reason to try to do in poor Luis. Maybe there's someone else Luis saw — or who thinks Luis saw him."

"As usual, your impeccable logic wins. So, when do we hog tie and brand that doggie?"

"To use your analogy, we still have to cut him out of the herd." Diega said as she exited the Jeep. "But I'm working on that."

Walkers, skaters, bicyclists, camera-toting tourists, and the occasional mime crowded the sidewalk of Venice Beach. Painters, fortunetellers, musicians, jewelry makers, political pontificators, and panhandlers lined the ocean side of the cement walkway, each hawking their wares and their pleas. The land side of the walkway consisted of established storefronts offering garish T-shirts, luggage, permanent and henna tattoos, sun dresses, leather goods, cheap sunglasses, swimwear, massages, and food. The calls of the seagulls were overridden by the cacophony of humans.

Diega and Tully headed for their favorite outdoor café, expertly wending their way through the crowds. Cool breezes chilled the women as they hurried along the walkway. Despite the weather, they decided to snag a table on the boardwalk where they could watch the passing scene without having to bob and weave.

After placing her order, Tully slid sunglasses onto her patrician nose and stared out at the crowds. "You'd think nobody had ever seen a Michael Jackson impersonator," she said, nodding at the three dozen people huddled around a young black man lip-syncing to a CD.

"Be glad the chainsaw juggler isn't here. That noise always gave me a headache."

Despite the sunglasses, Diega could tell her friend was eyeing a young woman with streamers woven into her long, brunette hair. The young woman was eyeing back.

Diega poked Tully. "Robbing the cradle now?"

Tully raised an eyebrow. "Me? How about you and that Erin kid? What's up with that?"

"I don't know if anything's up with that. Between her mom and her cancer, she's a little preoccupied."

In a rare turn of practicality, Tully asked, "Does she have health insurance?"

"She's not sure. Her job let her pay into her health benefits when she took a leave, but the leave is up in two more weeks and she probably won't be able to return to work. At least not right away."

Their conversation was interrupted by singing. A piano and pianist rolled slowly by on a flatbed dolly pulled by three men in tights and Renaissance costumes. They were followed by a group of a dozen men and women singing and passing out leaflets. One of the women stopped by their table and, without missing a note, handed them a flyer announcing a musical production.

Diega took the missive, then raised her sunglasses for a better look at the raven-haired woman. "Rita?"

Rita Morgan stopped singing and stared back at Diega. "Oh my God." She glanced around quickly. "Look, don't tell anyone at school. Please." She ran to catch up with the rest of her troupe.

Diega stared after Rita, but addressed Tully. "How hard would it be for an actress to look hysterical?"

Chapter Twenty-two

AS SOON AS Tully dropped her off after breakfast, Diega checked her telephone answering machine. To her surprise, Kathy Henshaw, Vista Elementary's former secretary, had left her a message. After a rambling greeting and expressions of joy over reconnecting with Diega, Kathy mentioned a news item she had heard about Zeke's son disappearing.

"Always knew that kid would come to no good," Kathy's voice related. "Couple of times Zeke came to see Rita at Vista last year. Sonny boy tracked him down. Hit his dad up for money right in front of me. Figured it was for drugs, but maybe he had other problems, too. Zeke never saw it. Just paid him and sent him away."

Diega stared at the wall. How strange it was that Kathy seemed to know that Rita and Zeke had been an item while she had no clue at all. Diega could not decide if that meant she needed to pay more attention to staff room gossip or if ignorance was bliss. She wondered how serious an affair it was with the two of them.

Diega switched her thoughts to Zeke's son. If Kathy was right and Wayne needed money for drugs, maybe he had a reason to emulate his father's less savory activities. If Wayne's run-in with the man in black at the club was any indication, he had already tried to emulate his father's venture into usury, so why not other areas of illegal income? Not that Wayne would have the inside power that his father had to extort money from businesses that had dealings with the school district, but was it such a leap to go from drug user to drug dealer? Diega figured if that was the road Wayne had taken, the police would only find bits of Wayne's body. Gangs were not tolerant of outsiders taking over their business.

Diega pushed the thought of yet another bleeding body aside and reached for the phone. Her uncle answered on the third ring.

"Uncle Juan, I'm hoping you could do me a favor." She explained about Wayne's disappearance and her observation of his exchange with Carl, the moneylender, at the Triple Aces. Then she made her request.

"So you want me to check with the loan sharks at the other clubs and see if this Wayne Chambers fellow has been to see them?"

"If you don't mind," Diega said.

"Mind? Mi hija, you have made my day."

Diega's next telephone call was to Detective Theophilus. Although she did not receive as warm a welcome as she had from her uncle, Diega plunged into her story, wrapping up with, "So Zeke Chambers seems to have had an affair with Rita Morgan."

Theophilus grunted. "I know. They broke it off about nine months ago. Amicably from all accounts."

Diega once again felt deflated. "Why do I keep telling you things? You already know them."

"Someday, you're going to give me a tidbit I haven't gleaned yet. And believe me," he said, sounding weary, "I'm ready for a break in this case." He cleared his throat. "By the way, do you remember how Ms. Morgan wore her hair last year?"

"I hate to tell you, but the fashion gene never made its way into my DNA. Why?"

"Evidently, she had short, curly hair such as yours. And she's about the same height and complexion, too. Well, if you don't count the fact that I'm sure you tan more easily than she does."

An image formed of Rita at the student-teacher softball game last June. Dark, curly hair framed her face. The connection clicked. "Wayne's ID of me at their house. It was Rita."

Theophilus did not respond directly. "Make sure to keep me informed. Even if I've already heard it, it's nice to get confirmation."

"So I'm your fact-checker."

"Ah, Ms. DelValle, you are so much more." Theophilus chuckled as he hung up.

DIEGA JOGGED UP the steep and winding path leading from the Griffith Observatory parking lot. She pushed her body up the trail and over a hilltop. At the crest of the hill, she bent over, panting, to catch her breath. Uphill running had not been in her regimen lately, and she felt her heart and lungs painfully complaining. The panoramic view of the skyscrapers of downtown Los Angeles did not capture her attention until her heartbeat settled into a more regular rhythm.

Collapsing onto a concrete bench, Diega sipped her water and contemplated the late winter landscape in front of her. Although the winter rains had been few, the pines were deep green and filled with cones. The chaparral covering the hillside had sprouting shoots that gave promise of the greening to come. Diega breathed the fresh air as she lazily observed the many other hearty souls who had made the afternoon climb to the overlook. To her, they all had the look of joy and peace that fills nature lovers on a day that can be comfortably enjoyed outdoors. She had the wry thought that this should be a time of contentment rather than a conflicted moment of worry over Erin's health and confusion around Zeke's murder. Once again she felt odd-woman-out with the world.

"Oh my goodness. Are you following me?" Megan plopped herself beside Diega. She poked a finger in Diega's arm. "Joking. If anyone was following anyone it would be me following you since you got up here first. Isn't that right?"

Before Diega could start a reply, her mentee's uncensored thoughts flowed forth. Obviously, the climb had not left the younger woman breathless.

"It's funny because I was talking to Jim yesterday about exercising and everything. He said he's not much on aerobic activities. He didn't have to tell me that. I mean, look at his paunch. Of course, with the weird hours he's been putting in at school, I'd be surprised if he had time to do anything else. I mean, last month he was there really late almost every night and, a few weeks ago, I came in on a Saturday morning because I had forgotten my umbrella and it was supposed to rain. Of course, you know how that is in California. They predict rain, but it hardly ever does. But it's better to be prepared. Anyway, I saw Jim's classroom door open, so I thought I'd say hi. He was searching through his desk and he jumped so high when I walked in, I thought he'd keel over right then. You know, a man his age can't be too careful. I think that's why I brought up exercise. Maybe, subconsciously, I wanted to encourage him. Anyway, he mentioned this hike, and it reminded me that I hadn't been up here in a long time, so here I am."

Megan looked more pleased with herself than with the view, and Diega was more interested in trying to figure out what Jim had been doing at school on a weekend than with whatever else might be running through Megan's vacant mind, so she did not bother replying.

Diega's silence did not seem to deter Megan. She was soon off on another tangent. "I haven't seen you at the Point before. It's one of my favorite runs. Walking to school is fine for a little stretch each day, but I need my cardio, too." Megan patted her forehead with a bandana. "Did you know Sally walks to school sometimes? I mean, her house is miles and miles away. Guess she worries about keeping her figure. Her husband isn't exactly a hunk, but even balding men can find younger women and I've heard he's open to the possibility, if you know what I mean. Or maybe she was keeping in shape to try to hold on to Zeke. You'd think a woman her age would get too tired to hold down a job and juggle two men at the same time."

Megan pulled on the pink elastic tie holding her ponytail together. "Not that the extra loving seems to have softened her any. She was really kind of nasty about that science lesson the other day. Sally made it clear that she was not impressed." Megan gave Diega a mournful look. "I did everything you said. I even told her that the whole thing was your lesson, but it didn't seem to make any difference." Her face brightened. "Of course, now that she's been arrested, she probably won't be principal much longer. I mean, I'll have grounds to dispute her evaluation, at least, won't I?"

Diega was torn between throwing herself over the cliff to escape Megan and giving into temptation and loosening her own tongue. Temptation won. "Someone you know has been accused of assaulting Luis and all you can think of is your evaluation?" Diega hauled herself to her feet. She glared down at Megan's pixie face. "If you paid as much attention to your teaching as you do to other people's lives, you wouldn't have to worry about your evaluation because you'd finally be doing a decent job."

Diega did not wait to see Megan's reaction. She merely jogged back down the trail.

Megan's yell was still audible to her halfway down the first switchback. "At least I'm not the one sucking up to the principal through her daughter."

"I'M SURPRISED YOU didn't fatten her lip." Tully's snort was clear over the phone line. "What good are all those kickboxing lessons you take if you don't put them into practice every once in a while?"

"Believe me, I briefly considered the possibility." Diega held her cell phone to her ear as she sat in her car in the observatory parking lot. "I needed to vent before I took out my aggressions on whoever happened to be sharing the road with me on the way home."

"Good thing you caught me. If you got into a wreck over this investigation, Jenny would never speak to either of us again."

"I hardly think Megan's self-centered idiocy counts as part of the investigation, as you put it, but you're probably right about Jenny. She has no sense of humor about some things." Diega leaned against the headrest. "Shit. Jenny. I forgot to check with her about Zeke's past. Maybe I'll give her a call."

"Do that, 'cause I've got to change and pick up Gina for dinner."

"Hmm. Three dinner dates in a row. That's even more serious than supplying a backyard for her kid."

Tully snorted again. "You watch yourself with little miss principal's daughter. That's one I could see hog tying you into matrimony in no time."

Tully's mention of Erin made Diega think of giving her a call. However, knowing she had nothing new to say, nothing to report, caused Diega to return to her original intention of phoning Jenny instead. Jenny answered on the third ring. To Diega's relief, Jenny sounded relaxed rather than stressed.

"Everything's going well here. I've got the room cleared out and the closet emptied. I've decided against a garage sale. Instead, I'm just going to dump all the excess off at one of the local thrift stores."

Diega reminded Jenny of her promise to check on Zeke's previous employment. To Diega's relief, Jenny had not forgotten. She waited while Jenny turned on her fax machine and checked for a report from her friend, Ray, who was her source.

Jenny was soon back on the line. She summarized as she skimmed what she described as an unusually long letter. "Ray says your guy worked for two other school districts before heading out to Glendale. He had his administrative credential even before he started teaching. Isn't that unusual?"

"A little. But it tells you where his heart was from the beginning."

"Anyway, his first job was as a special ed teacher, but he managed to work his way into administration within five years. Went up in rank before he jumped ship and hired on at another district. In that district, Chambers was the assistant superintendent in charge of district contracts with outside vendors." Jenny paused and Diega presumed she was reading since the silence lasted several seconds. "I'm not sure exactly what Ray means by this, but he says Zeke Chambers left that district in the middle of the school year and that he and the district issued a joint statement saying that he was leaving for personal health reasons."

Diega chewed her lip as she considered the possibilities. "It's a little strange to leave a school position anytime other than at the end of the school year, unless, maybe you were retiring. Could be he really was sick."

"Could also be that he was caught with his hand in the cookie jar, but the district didn't have enough to press charges."

"True. Sometimes they even buy someone out of their contract if they want the person gone bad enough."

"No mention of that," Jenny said. "Wouldn't you think Glendale would have checked on that before hiring him?"

Diega sighed. "If you want someone gone, you usually don't say anything negative about the person if another entity comes asking. Especially if they might hire your problem away."

"That's sick."

"True, but it's been known to happen."

"Any way to find out the truth?"

Diega started her car before she answered. "I can't. But I think I know someone who can."

Chapter Twenty-three

AS SOON AS she returned home, Diega telephoned Detective Theophilus. "One more tidbit to throw your way, even though you probably already know it." Diega went on to describe Zeke Chambers's abrupt departure from his last school district. She could hear Theophilus scribbling as she talked.

"Did your friend say there was any hint of misappropriation of funds or kickback complaints?"

"None that her source knew of. But I'd imagine they'd keep that as quiet as possible. No district wants that kind of press."

Theophilus cleared his throat. "You wouldn't want to tell me the name of this source, would you? It might save me time checking up on this."

"No can do. Mainly, because I don't know. And I don't want to inadvertently get someone in trouble who was doing me a favor. But I'm guessing you'll have your own sources to verify this."

"Well, congratulations. This is something we didn't catch. Thanks for the heads-up."

"Aren't you going to tell me to keep out of things now?"

His chuckle was loud in the receiver. "Would it do any good? Do me a favor and keep me up to date."

Diega had tried to get information in return for what she had given him, but he had merely laughed again and hung up. She had never run into such a jolly policeman before.

A Sunday night at home alone (if one could be excused for not counting the cats) suddenly did not appeal to Diega. She showered, changed into a navy blue sweater and black jeans, and drove over to the Triple Aces Club.

Carl, clad in what Diega had to assume was his usual black outfit, was sitting in the bar lounge of the club talking with another man who was dressed much more casually in jeans and a polo shirt. Diega witnessed Carl handing the man an envelope. When the man got up and returned to the casino, Diega slid onto the barstool.

Diega noted his broad forehead and wide cheekbones. She decided that somewhere in his ancestry a Native American passed by. Carl notice her perusal of him and raised an expressive, black eyebrow.

"Can I buy you a drink?" Diega asked Carl.

Carl's eyes swept Diega's body. "You're not my usual type."

"That makes us even. But I have some questions that only you can answer."

Carl swung his eyes around the sparsely populated bar before looking at Diega again. He shrugged. "What can I do for you?"

"I understand you lend money."

A blasé look entered Carl's eyes. "I sometimes do favors for friends."

"For a price."

Carl shrugged. "My friends like to show their appreciation. Who am I to turn down their generosity?"

"Look, I'm not the police. I'm not a private detective. And I'm not looking for trouble. All I want to know is how Zeke Chambers played into all this."

Carl clinked the ice in his glass. "I've seen you here before. Who did you come with?"

"Juan DelValle. He's my uncle."

"Juan is not a friend of mine."

"I know. He doesn't need loans. But, unless I'm mistaken, neither did Zeke. And yet you did business with him."

Carl slowly slid his glass in a circle along the polished bar top. "I did not do business with Zeke. He wanted to do business with me and I declined."

"Zeke wanted to lend you money?"

Carl barked a laugh. "Not exactly. Zeke wanted to start loaning money to his friends, something entirely legal and noble, you understand. But he didn't want them to know the money was coming from him. So he asked me if I would front some loans for some friends of his."

"So he wanted to piggyback on your network? He supplied the money and you supplied the collection process?"

"Something along those lines."

Diega thought about the potential profit in such a deal. "What's the going interest rate for a loan nowadays?"

Carl shrugged. "It depends upon the client. Between twenty and thirty percent is usual."

"A year?"

"A week."

Diega thought about the rate of interest her savings account earned and converted it to a weekly percentage. The difference was staggering. "So why did you turn down Zeke's offer?"

"My dear woman, Zeke is not the first person who viewed my business as an easy way to make money, which, I must say, it is not. Defaults are frequent and expensive, which is exactly why the rates are so high. Gamblers, you know, are not always the most trustworthy of individuals. However, I have no need of another supply of money," Carl said, smiling in a chilling fashion. "Which is exactly what I told your friend Zeke."

Carl grabbed his almost-empty glass and sauntered over to a table by the corner where two hulking men rose to greet him. They looked to Diega to be the same bulked-up men who had flanked Carl during his argument with Wayne.

Diega ordered a vodka gimlet and watched as Carl and the two men conversed for a minute. Even though her mind was elsewhere, she noticed one of Carl's musclemen turn and stare at her. When he turned away again, her thoughts went back to Carl's connection to Zeke. If Zeke truly had not been part of the loan sharking business then why did his son think he was? Then again, Diega thought as she squinted at Carl's back, maybe Zeke really had given Carl money to lend. Now that Zeke was dead, Carl could deny the whole thing and keep the cash. Not that there was any way anyone could prove it. She sipped her tangy drink and realized she had gained one more suspect.

A light tap on her shoulder caused Diega to spin around on the bar stool.

Honey Wong took the seat beside her and waved at the bartender. After giving her order for a bourbon and seven, Honey said, "Juan gave me the idea you weren't a gambler. Are you keeping secrets from him?"

"Only that I'm a drinker. He still thinks of me as being pure and innocent."

Honey's laugh was deep and sultry. Her drink arrived, but she did not touch it. "I saw you talking with Carl. Do you know him?"

Diega shrugged. "Only by reputation."

"Believe me, you don't want to get to know that son of a bitch." Honey swirled her drink in the tall glass. "Look, if you need money, Carl is not the right way to get it. He's a nasty piece of work. I'm sure your uncle would loan you some, no matter what the problem. He seems awfully fond of you, and Juan doesn't gush about too many people."

"Thanks, but I'm not hard up for cash. I was only checking on who Carl might have done business with."

Honey snorted. "Hell, half the club. Even some of the big time players. But if you're trying to get Carl to name names, you'll fail. That's part of what the interest pays for: his silence."

Diega studied Honey's wide cheeks, up-slanted obsidian eyes, and full lips which were currently stretched into a grimace. No secrets were exposed by her face. "How much did you borrow from him?"

"Not me. My sister. She used to be the pretty one." Honey ran her finger around the rim of the glass. "At least she stays away from the tables now. See, that's the exchange. Carl writes off your debt because you pay in blood and your future credit dries up completely."

Diega did not think she wanted details. "If he's such a nasty guy, why doesn't someone else step in with better terms and a kinder, gentler approach to collections? Seems like the business would all flow to the new person."

"You may drink, but you are still sweet and innocent." Honey patted Diega on the cheek. "Carl is part of the L.A. area Mafia. Not what they call themselves, but no matter. About a year ago, George, a young, cocky, black guy, tried what you said. Undercut Carl's prices and promised limited violence if you didn't pay." Honey let her eyes drift off to the back of the bar. "Within a week, George's collection boys had all disappeared. I heard later that George's legs were crushed so badly he had to have them amputated. Funny thing is, the police never found out who did it."

Diega swiveled to look at Carl's back again. She had a bad feeling about Zeke's son if he had tried to worm his way into the money lending underground.

Chapter Twenty-four

DIEGA LEFT THE Triple Aces Club around the time her uncle would probably have arrived, namely ten o'clock. She had self-parked, so the walk across dozens of rows of automobiles gave her time to reflect on Honey's tale. Had Zeke tried to undercut Carl? If so, would Carl have sent his thugs to Vista to kill Zeke?

A Mafia hit at an elementary school? Diega could not stretch her imagination far enough to envision that scenario. She was back to musing over who would know that Zeke would be at Vista. That list seemed to be very short. In fact, it was nearly non-existent as far as her investigation had discovered.

Tires squealed behind Diega. She whirled around and saw a dark green car speeding down the roadway toward her. Before she could leap to the side, a hand grasped her arm and flung her against a car hood. The green car raced by, missing her by inches. It skidded around a corner and screamed into the street before Diega could register anything about it or the driver.

Diega took stock of her body parts before turning to her rescuer. To her astonishment, Detective Theophilus was the one at her side, talking rapidly into his phone.

As he flipped it shut, Theophilus looked at Diega and said, "What have you done now to piss someone off?"

"Me? Did you see the way that guy was weaving? I bet his blood test results would rival Robert Downey, Jr's."

"I got the license plate. We'll find the guy."

A crowd had formed around them. Diega listened as two men presented conflicting versions of the event to a security guard. A woman approached Diega and offered to drive her to the hospital, but Diega declined.

As Theophilus dealt with both the onlookers and the guards, Diega found her brain able to work again. She replayed the scene of the car coming at her. When the detective came to her side again, she said, "You'll only find the driver if he's a drunk. If he's not a drunk, I'd wager the car was stolen."

"Coming around to my way of thinking? So who did you antagonize in there?"

Diega leaned against the car where the detective had thrown her. She described her conversation with Carl and with Honey.

Theophilus looked grim by the end of her recitation. "I was stopping by to chat with Mr. Carl Randolph anyway. This may add a new item to the discussion." He unlocked the door to the car Diega was leaning on and extracted a large notebook from the back seat.

Diega noticed the car fell into the less well-maintained category of vehicles in the lot. "Your department isn't spending a lot on keeping up their cars nowadays, are they?"

"Cutbacks are everywhere," Theophilus said as he closed and locked the door. "But this happens to be my own."

Diega felt redness creep up her cheeks. "Sorry."

Theophilus shrugged. "The price of divorce. I'd rather my kids had new clothes than my car have a paint job."

"Goodness. A guy with scruples as well as being a hero. How do you keep the women away?"

"Something about being a cop seems to directly cancel any pheromones I might give off."

"Being a teacher can have that same effect. By the way, I neglected to thank you. I do appreciate you preventing me from becoming roadkill."

Theophilus tipped an imaginary hat. "Just doing my job, ma'am. Now let me walk you to your car. Once I see you safely drive away, I'll get back to what I came here to do."

TULLY SNORTED INTO the phone. "That good ol' boy seems to be cropping up a might too often for my taste. How'd the Greek know you'd be at the poker club?"

The crunching sound over the receiver gave Diega the impression she had interrupted Tully's after-dinner snack time. "Are those chips or cookies you're indulging in?"

"Never mind what I'm eating. Tell me why you think the local payday lender decided to take you out."

"Since he didn't seem to mind talking to me, I can only think that he saw me with Honey and that somehow riled him."

"But this poker buddy of your uncle didn't tell you anything new, did she?"

"No. But would Carl know that? Maybe he thinks Honey knows something really damaging about him."

A second snort greeted that suggestion. "In that case, he'd send the car after her, not you."

Diega chewed over that thought while Tully chewed on her snack.

"Anyway," Tully said, "I heard that your boy, Zeke, had feelers out for financial backers. Friend of mine puts together financing for films. Word was that Zeke was approaching everybody but banks for a wad of cash. He was pushing for a large chunk of change with a promise of repayment with more than the going rate of interest within a year."

"Sounds like he was closing in on a big deal with an even bigger payoff." Diega squinted at the wall, recalling her conversation with the hospitalized Harrison who had probably caught the wrong end of a deal with the man in black. "Why do you suppose Harrison tried to convince me that Zeke was the cash behind Carl?"

A final crunch and the rustle of a bag indicated to Diega that Tully's indulgence was at an end. "Maybe," Tully said, when the crackling had died away, "our wayward teacher thought the Italian branch of Carl's family might object to him discussing their business dealings with you."

"Maybe they did," said Diega, thinking of the evening's misadventure. "Not Harrison, since he didn't, but Honey and Carl both talked with me. Maybe someone wasn't happy about that." A yawn bubbled up and overtook her. "It's so frustrating that none of this seems to point to why Zeke needed money and who might have killed him, but I'm calling it a night."

"I'd say 'sweet dreams,' but I'm betting yours will border on the homicidal side."

AT 7:45 MONDAY morning, Diega strode up the ramp leading to the temporary bungalow that Rita's class now occupied. She had disturbed the cats all night by muttering and tossing, deciding what to do. Both BB and Sherwood ended up deserting her for their carpeted penthouse atop the scratching post where they obviously felt they could get a better night's sleep. She might have joined them had there been room.

The door to the bungalow was open, so Diega walked in. Rita was facing the back of the classroom and leapt when Diega cleared her throat.

"Diega, you nearly killed me," she said, with her right hand flat against her well-endowed chest.

Diega had never really looked at Rita in terms of rating her attractiveness. Although not at all to her taste, Rita, Diega realized, was actually an attractive woman. Her wide eyes, generously enhanced with makeup, and regular features gave her an open, friendly look. At least they would have if Rita had not been scowling at her.

"Is there something you wanted or were you merely trying to jump-start my heart?"

"I was watching a Burbank Board of Education meeting from last year. Zeke spoke at it. Do you remember?"

Rita grabbed a stack of neatly piled papers on her desk and started to unnecessarily straighten them. "Why would I know anything about the Burbank Board of Ed? I don't even pay attention to those clowns who think they know something about running this city's schools."

"That's why I thought it was strange to see you in the audience."

Rita stopped tapping the edges of the papers. She started twisting the rings on her fingers instead. She looked up at Diega. "I remember now. I did go to one because they were discussing something about reading. It was a program that a friend of mine was interested in."

Diega raised an eyebrow. "Might that friend have been Zeke Chambers?"

"Whatever would give you that idea?" Rita glanced at her wristwatch. "I can't talk anymore. I need to get ready for class." She turned and began writing on the board.

Realizing she would get no more that day, Diega headed back to her own classroom. Upon entering the building, she spotted her mentee, Megan. Before Megan could get a chance to get her mouth in gear, Diega asked, "Did you ever see Zeke Chambers hanging around Rita's room?"

Megan seemed to hold no grudge against Diega for yesterday's outburst since she answered readily. "Not lately, if that's what you mean." She drew her hair over her shoulder and ran her fingers through it. "After all, they've been old news for a long time."

"They? You mean Zeke and Rita?"

"Sure. Everyone knows Zeke had a fling with Rita. I think he felt sorry for her. After all, an older woman like that throwing herself at a good-looking man like Zeke. It was pitiful." Megan obviously warmed to her tale as she stopped combing her hair and leaned closer to Diega. "You know, she followed him everywhere. I heard that she even went to his house once asking for him. Maybe she really hadn't given up on him." She shook her head. "It's so sad when women get desperate, isn't it?"

"You said 'everybody' knew this?"

"Sure. It was last year and I was new, but I still heard the gossip. Don't you ever listen in the teachers' lounge? You'd be surprised at what you'd learn."

Chapter Twenty-five

"NO, IT WASN'T Luis who told me about Zeke being here when Sally wasn't. A group was talking about it in the teacher's lounge. At least, that's what Cindy said. She heard the gossip from them and then she told me. Maybe she knows who was in that group of chitchatters, but I sure don't." Jim Tolkien had followed her into Room Five when she returned following her unedifying discussion with Rita. He leaned against her desk, foot swinging rapidly back and forth. Diega knew it was Jim's way of relieving tension, but some days it irritated her.

Today was one of those days.

Diega had hoped Jim could pinpoint who had actually seen Zeke Chambers roaming the hallways of Vista Elementary. No such luck. Unsubstantiated rumors with no specific source only muddied the Mississippi, a body of water needing no help in that direction.

"Did Cindy happen to mention who started the conversation?"

Jim shrugged. "I never thought to ask." He straightened. "But I did hear that Zeke was leaving the GUSD. He had a very lucrative job offer from a private school. So it looks like he had stolen all the information he needed from Glendale and was moving onto greener turf."

Ignoring Jim's conspiracy theory, Diega asked, "Was the company Brighter Days?"

"No. Cindy heard from Sherry—or was it Ruth?—that it was the one that recently opened a charter school in Chatsworth."

Diega wondered if that was the stiff price Zeke had exacted from Gwen Gunther.

When Jim finally wandered off to set up his own classroom, Diega began to pull out the reading materials for her first lesson. A quiet cough stopped her.

"Sorry to interrupt."

Erin's voice made Diega close her eyes for a moment before turning to face her with what she hoped was a welcoming smile. "You are definitely not an interruption. You can stop by anytime."

Erin smiled in return. "After Saturday, I wasn't sure you ever wanted to see me again, but I talked with my dad and I thought you'd like to know some things."

Diega tilted her head toward a side chair and Erin perched on the edge.

"First of all, Dad said that my mom and Zeke had no appointments together that week at all. In fact, Mom had been in touch with the superintendent asking to be taken off the assignment. So Zeke really had no legit reason for being at Vista that day."

An affair with your mother would not usually be considered a legitimate reason, Diega wanted to say, but thought better of it. Instead she said, "How does your dad know this?"

"Well, duh. They do talk. At least they did before all of this blew up." Erin blew out air. "This is harder than I thought it would be."

"Take your time. I have," Diega looked up at the black hands of the round classroom clock, "fourteen minutes before my cherubs arrive."

"Well, I had a more elaborate apology prepared, but I guess I'll give you the short version." Erin stood. "I'm sorry I yelled at you and I'm sorry I didn't listen to you about what I did and how my parents would feel. Mom was released late yesterday and she gave me the strongest lecture I've gotten from her since I was eleven and tried to free the lobsters from the tank at our local seafood restaurant."

Diega could not hold back a grin. "I'm sorry you got caught." At Erin's confused look, Diega added, "The lobsters, not your confession about Zeke."

Erin nodded and started to leave. Diega reached out and touched her sleeve.

When Erin looked up at her face, Diega said, "If you're free, how about dinner tonight? No lobsters, but I grill a great salmon."

Erin smiled. "Throw in some veggies and I'm there."

KNOWING SHE WOULD burst if she couldn't talk over everything before her dinner date with Erin, Diega contacted Felicia for a long-overdue haircut and confab. Felicia seemed more than willing to set aside her packing to clip and chat.

"In fact," Felicia had said over the telephone, "I picked up the juiciest bit of information."

Visions of hospitals, surgeries, and gory medical procedures flowed through Diega's mind as she drove up Colorado Boulevard after school. She turned left and headed up into the foothills. Felicia had a place in the last apartment building on the street. Past Felicia's abode were single-family homes and spectacular mountain views.

Sealed cardboard boxes were stacked along the walls of the empty living room. More boxes, some taped closed and some half-filled, sat on the kitchen countertops.

Felicia greeted Diega with a hug. "Glad you called. I needed a break and it sounds like you need to talk. So give."

Diega plopped into the dentist chair Felicia had installed in an alcove of her kitchen for her private hair clients. As Felicia wrapped a cape around her shoulders, Diega told her about Erin and the recurrence of the cancer.

Felicia's eyes immediately filled with tears. "Oh that poor child. Have you talked with Jenny?"

Diega nodded. "Tully suggested that, too. Jenny said she'd check out some new therapies at the City of Hope and let us know about any cancer trials and such."

Diega swiveled the chair so that she could see out the window. She needed to move her mind off of Erin's fate and onto something, anything, else. She took a deep breath then spent a moment admiring Felicia's view of the apartment's lush garden. "Aren't you going to miss this when you move in with Jenny?" she asked with a nod at the greenery.

Felicia waved her scissors toward the picture window. "This can be duplicated. Jenny can't." She put her hands on her hips and regarded Diega sternly. "Honey child," she said in her best Georgian accent, "even you know that love is more important than location. Wouldn't matter if Jenny lived in a tree, I'd be happy sitting on a limb with her."

"K-I-S-S-I-N-G?"

"Sure wouldn't be room on a branch for much more than that." Felicia pulled her fingers through Diega's hair. "Are you planning on swinging from a tree branch with your new little cutie?"

"She has cancer. I think she's got her mind on other things at the moment."

"Sometimes life has a way of bringing us things we didn't know we wanted or needed." Felicia snipped around Diega's right ear. "It took me some time to realize that I love Jenny, the person, not the package she comes in. It's been a struggle especially since I don't think I would have fallen for her when she was Jimmy, if you know what I mean. Which would have been a real tragedy since I would have missed out on having this incredible person in my life."

Diega ventured a translation. "It's the essence of the person, not the vessel?"

"Amen, sister."

"But Erin could be dying." The comment erupted from Diega without thought or edit. As soon as it burst from her lips, she knew that it was the core of her concern.

Felicia stopped cutting and swung the chair around so that Diega faced her. "Dee, honey, I know that must be scarier than all get-out." She tilted her head and waited until she had caught Diega's eye before continuing. "As much as we don't like to think about it, we are all dying. From the moment that we're born. Only the good Lord knows how much time any of us have, and She's not telling." Felicia tapped Diega on the nose. "But, sweetheart, the way you go around getting mixed up in murders and such, there's no guarantee that your life span is going to exceed hers."

Diega nodded, not trusting her voice.

Felicia must have sensed Diega's discomfort. She spun Diega around again and proceeded with the haircut. Silence prevailed for several minutes before Felicia switched the subject. "I heard something in the newsroom that I thought you might like to know."

"About Zeke?"

"Not directly. But you mentioned that friend of yours. Gwen? Doesn't she run a charter school?"

"Yeah. A Plus Academies. She's got them in a lot of cities now."

"Maybe not for much longer," Felicia said, as she ran a comb through Diega's curls. She began a rhythmic snip and comb routine as she talked. "One of the reporters was telling me that some of the charter schools in the area are in big trouble. Not only are the kids' test scores not so hot, but there's talk of the state auditing their finances."

Diega swiveled her eyes in Felicia's direction since she could not move her whole head without a coiffure disaster. "Did this reporter say which ones are involved?"

Felicia's snipping never skipped a beat. "He mentioned a couple, but I don't remember if your friend's group was one of them. I can ask if you want me to. But there's one other interesting fact." Felicia stopped and moved in front of Diega. She grabbed Diega's chin and moved her head from side to side. "Think I can talk you into a new look?"

"No, but you can finish your story."

Felicia shook her head in a pitying way. "Someday you are going to get sick of looking into the mirror and seeing that same old you. Anyway," she said, picking up her scissors again, "because of all this hoopla, there's talk in the legislature about making it harder to form new charter schools. And wasn't that what our not-so-dearly departed wanted to do? Looks like his heirs are going to have to move fast or they're going to lose their chance at the golden ring of public education funding."

Felicia swept the cape from around Diega's neck. She fluffed Diega's hair with her fingers and said, "I wish the newscasters were as easy as you are to work with. Last night Les, the weatherman, kept turning his head to talk to everyone who wandered by and then complained when his cut was shorter on one side." She sniffed. "I told him to keep his right side to the camera."

Chapter Twenty-six

THE OLD ABBA tune, "Money, Money, Money" played in Diega's head as she strolled the vegetable aisles of the grocery store. Money lending. Money borrowing. Possible embezzlement. A great, gushing need for money. Why would an assistant superintendent of a relatively small school district need so much money?

Diega picked over the bell peppers and zucchini as she pondered Zeke's activities. Gambling. Women. Education Edge. Unless Zeke was hiding a major gambling debt, the private charter school was the only part of his life that seemed to possibly need an infusion of cash. Or was it already up and running?Diega telephoned Gwen Guntherson as soon as she got home. "Tell me again about how charter schools get their money." Diega grabbed a notepad to jot down information as she listened.

"We're paid the same way a school district is, through average daily attendance. We don't always get the full amount because some districts charge administrative costs. And, of course, we have to pay rent to the district unless we own our own building."

"So you save by cutting out the unions."

"Now, Diega, we don't cut out the unions. Our teachers aren't covered by the collective bargaining agreements of the school district, but we pay health coverage and they can still opt into the state retirement system. We do lower costs in other ways. We see if we can provide services other than teaching at a lesser price by outsourcing them. Most of the outside companies we use are union shops."

"You end up making a profit."

Gwen laughed. "Hopefully, or I wouldn't have a salary. But that profit, as you call it, is overseen by the board of directors and goes back into the school. In some cases it goes as bonuses to our teachers — something you should keep in mind."

"Are your schools one of the ones the state is investigating?"

"Oh. So that's what's got you worried. Well, we've got no problems on that score. A Plus is not under suspicion of financial malpractice or anything else. We're fine. There are some companies out there who don't understand how important it is to keep careful financial records. Those are the ones the government is after."

Diega made a note to check out Gwen's claims. "What does it take to actually open a charter school?"

"No special qualifications. You have to make a plan and fill out an application." A worried tone entered Gwen's voice. "You're not thinking of striking out on your own, are you?"

"Nope. But Zeke Chambers was. About how much cash do you

think he would need as a starter fund?"

"That snake. So that's why he was asking so many questions. That smarmy sack of—" Gwen broke off, muttering. Finally, she asked, "Was he working on a single campus or a statewide system of campuses?"

"According to what I've read, he was going for multiple campuses."

"Then he'd need buildings or rental agreements along with the start-up funds since we're only paid quarterly. Hmm. Let me think."

The amount Gwen finally named widened Diega's eyes and evoked a silent whistle from her lips. She thanked Gwen for her help, but she sensed Gwen was not really listening. Diega heard more of Gwen's mutterings about Zeke's lack of ethics before she hung up.

Noting the time, Diega turned on the radio for company and started to prepare the cedar plank and season the salmon. As she oiled the plank, her mind returned to Zeke and his pursuit of money. If Education Edge was truly driving his need for cash, she could see not wanting to possibly bankrupt his family in search of a dream. He would need backers or a separate stream of financing.

Did Zeke's greed tick off one of the businesses he was pressing for money? Maybe Gwen lied about not paying Zeke bribes to support her charter school effort in Glendale. If she was paying him off, maybe she got tired of it. Or if her business was one of the companies the state was going after, she might have needed to expand quickly. In that case, if Zeke was the one block to her ambitions, how tempting would it be to permanently remove that block?

Of course, Diega reasoned, that might apply to any of the companies Zeke was bleeding. The idea of a business meeting, especially dirty business, fit in with the scenario of Zeke using Vista as neutral ground to make a deal. Diega wished she had access to Zeke's bank accounts. If she knew how much money he really had, that might help determine how much, if any, money he would need to open his fleet of schools.

The thought of Zeke's family made Diega consider Mrs. Chambers. Zeke was a serial cheater. Maybe she was kicking him out and that's why he needed the money. Maybe alimony and child support would strip him of his extra cash. Or maybe leaving him wasn't enough for his wife. Maybe she wanted revenge. But then, why would she come to the school to kill him? And it would not make sense for Zeke to have an appointment to see his wife.

Diega sliced the bell peppers into strips. The roar of a motorcycle from the street outside her home brought Zeke's son to mind. He certainly seemed capable of murderous anger. Perhaps he and his father had wrangled that morning and he had followed Zeke to Vista.

Diega narrowed her eyes as she visualized the scene. The angry son. The angrier father who had just had his nose broken. Would the son really help his dad mop up his bloody nose before taking him into another room to stab him?

Diega shook her head. A wife might, but not a son. Especially if Zeke said something to infuriate his wife right after she took care of him.

Diega started quartering the zucchini. As the vegetables blurred in her vision, Diega let her mind play with the concept of Sally as the killer. She fit the psychology. She would tend to Zeke's wounds, especially if he told her Patrick had clobbered him. She might even usher him into the room next door to get water. But why would she need to use Zeke's master key when she had one of her own? And what could Zeke have said that would cause Sally to pick up scissors and stab him? Maybe Sally had lied about not being involved with Zeke romantically. If so, maybe Zeke called off their affair. That might tempt her to jab something into his back. But why would they be meeting in a classroom rather that in her office? That would be less suspicious if anyone saw them together since they met in the office all the time.

Diega felt a throbbing in her own head. She felt sure she was missing something she had heard or seen, but could not call it to mind.

Finally, she gave in and cast Erin in the part of murderer. Diega doubted if Erin would make an appointment to see Zeke, so if she killed him it must have been a crime of opportunity. Maybe Erin wasn't lying about finding out about the affair through her father. Maybe she did follow her dad to Vista, saw the altercation, and decided to confront Zeke after her father left. She finds him bleeding in Diega's room. Why would she care for his wounds? Diega could see Erin picking up a book and smacking him then and there, but she could not see her escorting the man who was breaking up her parents' marriage into another room and soaking cold compresses for him.

As Diega tossed the vegetables in seasonings, olive oil, and balsamic vinegar, she heard the radio announcer read an ad for the revival of the play *Educating Rita*.

Rita, Diega thought. What about Rita? Zeke was, after all, killed in her room. That would explain why the killer had brought Zeke to that room. Did she wait until she heard noises in Diega's room before putting on a show of hysterics? She's an actress. She could pull it off. But what motive would Rita have? Her affair with Zeke was over long ago by all accounts.

Diega set the table. As she laid out the knives, she thought of poor Luis. Why would any of them try to kill Luis? They all could have explained away their presence if he had seen them.

Diega knew Agatha Christie's Hercule Poirot always said that psychology was the key to any murder. She was beginning to feel like she should have paid closer attention to that course in college.

DESPITE DIEGA'S BEST intentions, talk over dinner turned to Zeke and his murder and its aftermath.

"Since she was arrested, the Board has suspended Mom. She said she's going in tomorrow to clean out her office. Dad and I offered to help, but she wants to do it alone." Erin finished chewing on a grilled portabella mushroom before saying, "I've been going over and over it all in my head. I can't figure it out. My mom swears that Zeke had no business at Vista that morning. So why was he there?"

"Didn't she tell your dad that she had a meeting that morning?"

"Yeah. She was supposed to meet one of the counselors from her old school to talk over some issues on the grant, but he never showed. She called him later and he said he must have gotten his dates mixed up."

How convenient, Diega thought, but did not comment. She helped herself to another piece of sourdough bread instead.

Erin insisted on continuing the examination of the means, motive, and actions of the murder. Diega finally gave in and repeated much of what she had been ruminating on during the afternoon. This lasted through the end of dinner and the beginning of cleanup, something Erin insisted on helping with.

While carrying their dishes to the sink, Diega even told Erin of the suspicions she entertained about Erin herself.

Erin listened while rinsing the plates. She shook her hands and dried them on the blue towels beside the sink. "You really believe I'm capable of murder?" Erin crossed her muscular arms and gazed at Diega.

Diega shrugged. "You've got to admit it's a possibility. You're physically strong enough. Your dad had told you about his suspicions about an affair between your mom and Zeke so, as weak a motive as it is, you had a reason to want Zeke out of the way. Finally, you lied about when you returned from Europe. I'm not saying you've ever topped my list of suspects. I'm merely telling you how my mind has been working."

"You really think I could kill to protect someone I love?"

Diega nodded.

"You're absolutely right." Erin smiled and laced her arms around Diega's neck. "And don't you forget it," she said, pressing her lips against Diega's.

Chapter Twenty-seven

DIEGA CAUGHT HERSELF whistling as she wove through the parking lot of Vista Elementary the next morning. Grinning, she decided the heck with decorum and increased the volume of her musical efforts. Even the sight of Megan Beaker in the hallway did not pause her tune.

Megan did not seem to notice or care about Diega's mood. "I guess you're the only one who didn't catch the early bug today. I mean, you're always here by 7:30 and it's nearly 8:00. Even Jim's been in his classroom for quite a while, and Sally must have gotten up with the roosters. She was almost finished cleaning out her office when I got in at 7:15."

During this narrative, Diega managed to reach her classroom, unlock her door, and deposit her materials on her desk. Megan followed her in, motor mouth on full.

"I'm doing that lesson on prisms today. I have five that the students can share, but only four flashlights 'cause one of mine died. You have a penlight one, don't you?"

Diega vowed that not even Megan was going to ruin her good mood today. She pulled open the long, flat, top drawer where she kept her pencils, pens, erasers, and miscellaneous small hardware items sometimes needed for quick repairs.

"Eww," Megan said, pointing. "What's that yucky thing?"

The metal object was a key with a number and the words "Do Not Duplicate" stamped on it. Beside it lay a caked and stained embroidered handkerchief.

DIEGA STUDIED THE emptied principal's office. She had not realized what the personalized touches did to an otherwise bland space. The blank, plastered walls, bare bookshelves, and the polished desktop void of paper, calendars, and photos gave the room an abandoned air. Sally had even removed her philodendron and orchids. To Diega, it looked as if Sally did not plan on ever returning.

Detective Theophilus interrupted her musing by waving her into one of two matching chairs in front of the desk. To Diega's surprise, he chose the other one rather than Sally's swivel chair behind the desk.

"I've got my class coming in less than five minutes. I don't have time to go over this with you again. I told the whole story to the first two cops that arrived." Diega knew she was coming close to whining, but at that point she didn't care.

Detective Theophilus merely turned a page in his notebook.

Jim Tolkien stuck his head in the office door. "I'll pick up your little cherubs for you and take both classes out for a very early P.E."

"That's above and beyond, Jim. I'll make it up to you somehow."

"Aw, let me count the ways." Jim gave a wave and an evil grin.

Diega explained to the detective that with Sally on paid administrative leave, the school was without a principal and it was not standard operating procedure around Vista at the moment. "Eventually the district is going to notice us and do something, but until then, we are on our own."

Theophilus simply reiterated his original question. "Lead me through your arrival again."

While Diega reviewed her morning, she noticed he did not take notes. He only tapped his pencil and stared at Sally's desk.

"According to Ms. Beaker, you didn't seem surprised to see the key and handkerchief."

"Maybe because I was too stunned to react to her satisfaction. She certainly had enough of a reaction for both of us." Diega pulled at her nose in thought. "I saw initials embroidered on one corner. I think one was a Z."

No confirmation or denial came from the policeman.

"I imagine that's not too common an initial, and Zeke was a natty dresser, the kind who would carry an embroidered handkerchief. So I'm going out on a limb here and guess that it was Zeke's handkerchief. I'm also going to guess that stain was blood. His blood. Which would lead me to think that was Zeke's master key." It was Diega's turn to stare at the desk. "If that's the case, why is somebody out to frame me?"

The detective broke his silence. "It's too soon to know what the stain is or who the handkerchief belonged to."

Diega noticed Theophilus did not address the matter of the master key, which, with its imprinted number, had to be easily identifiable. But she did not press him.

The detective continued, "Since neither object was in that drawer when we searched your room after the murder, they've obviously been placed there at some later date. If these objects do have something to do with Mr. Chambers's murder, then someone might have made a clumsy attempt to frame you." His eyes studied Diega's face before adding, "Or it may be your very clever way of diverting attention away from the real killer."

DIEGA GAZED AT the tops of her student's heads. They were all actually concentrating on a math assignment despite holding class in the auditorium for the second time this month. Room Five had been declared off-limits again until the crime scene investigators finished checking for fingerprints or any other evidence relating to the Zeke Chambers murder that might have been secreted away. The substitute custodian did not have Luis's careful attention to detail, so this temporary setup was more ragtag than the one before, but it was functional.

Diega doubted the police would find anything in her room. She was sure the murderer wanted those objects to be seen. He or she wanted Diega to be caught with them. The gruesome thought overtook her that this was a lot better than having a letter opener shoved into her back.

She wondered how a day that had begun so well could go down in flames so quickly. The accompanying notion was, could it get any worse? Suddenly, worry turned to anger. She was damned if someone was going to screw up her life right now.

She scrounged for a piece of paper. Heading the columns WHO and WHEN, she listed every individual who was even peripherally involved in the case. On the WHEN side, she considered if and when each one of those people could have entered her room since about 3:00 yesterday until 8:00 this morning. Given the person had a master key and the building was not alarmed, the time frame was wide open. Each person's knowledge of where her room was also had to be evaluated. Chances were against someone like Carl and his poker club buddies, but Diega was not willing to rule them out.

Quiet talking brought Diega out of her reverie. Her class needed her attention again. She rose to continue the lesson, but her mind was fixed on revenge.

Chapter Twenty-eight

JIM WAS NOT in the teacher's lounge at lunch time. Diega tracked him down in his classroom where he sat hunched over sheets of paper spread across his desk. She knocked on the doorframe. "I wanted to thank you again for taking my class this morning."

Jim nodded, then spread his hands apart, indicating the papers. "I'd love to talk, but I'm on a bit of a deadline."

"Sorry. I'll catch you later."

Before Diega could leave, Jim said, "Wait. Why don't you sit down? I've been meaning to talk with you about this. And now is about as good a time as any." Jim rose and walked over to where Diega had taken a seat in a student's chair. He leaned on the desk next to her. "My friend Vince and I have been kicking this idea around for a while. I was going to invite you over for a glass of wine and feel you out about it, but what the hell."

Jim seemed embarrassed and excited at the same time. "You know I hate the way the Board runs the schools. They make asinine decisions about curriculum, textbooks, assignments. Basically everything. You know and I know that teachers could run a school better. We would make decisions based on the kids, not the politics."

Diega pointed to the pile of papers. "So you're writing a declaration of independence and starting a revolution?"

"Exactly. Well, almost." Jim paced the floor. "You've heard of charter schools, right? They're kind of the Wild West of education. Unfortunately, corporations are glomming on to them. But there are still independent schools that make a difference. Just think," Jim said, sliding into a seat beside Diega. "We could create courses of study that matter. Who needs grade levels and kids walking lockstep through a curriculum about old white men created by old white men? We need to be developing citizens of the world. We could teach the way kids should be taught. We could bring in the best and the brightest teachers who care about children and want to change the world." He threw his hands in the air. "It would be a revolution. What do you say? Are you on board?"

For the second time that day, Diega was stunned. "I'm blown away, Jim. How long have you been working on this?"

"Most of this school year. I've been researching the steps in creating a charter school and meeting with some of the parents I know who see eye-to-eye with me. I even talked with some former students. I had to understand what they wanted from schools, what they saw as needs that weren't being met."

"Doesn't it cost a ton of money?"

"It would if we were trying to set up a whole raft of schools, but I'm only talking about one kindergarten through fifth-grade school. The beauty is, the district has an unused building on the site of Kennedy Elementary. And, since the district isn't using that structure for classrooms, it's required to rent it to us for a nominal fee. We don't have to buy or renovate anything. The maximum government loan you can get wouldn't go far if you were setting up a bunch of campuses, but it will cover most of the rest of our startup expenses, which will mainly be salaries. Since we're only talking about eight teachers and a financial guru, it won't be much at all. And we could pay that loan off over five years. My brother-in-law is an investment banker. He's willing to back us with the rest of the money for a small rate of interest. He might even do the financials for us." He stalked to his desk and gathered the sheets together. "This is the proposal. I wanted to have it totally ready before talking to you, but..." He shoved the bundle at her. "Read it. Tell me what you think. I want to bring it before our Board of Education next month before some blood-sucking, soulless, corporate charter school monster comes and sweeps them off their feet."

Diega stared at the pile of papers, bemused. Promising to read them and get back to Jim by the beginning of the week, Diega added, "I'll drop these off back in the auditorium, then I need to grab some lunch."

As she reached the auditorium, she heard her cell phone ringing. For once she had brought it with her to work, but she was still not in the habit of carrying it with her at all times. She dug around her makeshift desk and found the phone.

Erin's voice caused a smile to erupt from Diega's face.

"Please thank Jenny for me for getting me that appointment with the City of Hope. They reviewed my files, and we went over their suggestions and options." Erin cleared her throat. "I'd be lying if I said there was a lot to choose from. It's somewhere between doing nothing or doing things that may prolong my life. No promises. No cures."

At that moment, Diega longed to be able to wrap her arms around Erin.

"Sorry to tell you this over the phone, but I wanted to tell you first. I'm heading home to talk with my parents." Erin's voice caught. "They don't know anything about this. Not the recurrence. Not the diagnosis. With all that's going on with Mom and all, I was hoping..."

"I'm guessing you need time with your folks tonight."

"I think you're right. Sorry to cancel out. I'd really like to see you, more than you know."

"Probably not as much as I want to be holding you right now, but I understand."

DIEGA STRETCHED OUT on her couch, clutching both cats to her.

Sherwood seemed delighted with the extra afternoon loving session. Beelzebub put up with it, however, Diega figured she was only biding her time before demanding dinner. The doorbell caused both kitties to leap from her stomach leaving skid marks on her skin from their claws.

Gently rubbing her injured abdomen, Diega peered through the peephole before opening the door to Jenny.

"I can't stay," Jenny said, carrying a tall reading lamp by its brass stem. "I'm only dropping off the furniture you loaned me. Here's the lamp. The chair's out in the car."

"Emptying the guest bedroom?"

Jenny nodded. "Almost done. Who knew that preparing for cohabitation would require so much weeding and cleaning?"

"Yet another reason no one shares this abode."

Jenny merely shook her head and asked, "Where do you want this?"

"Leave it here. I'll move it into my art room later. Let's get the chair together. I've got some room beside my car in the garage. It'll have to stay there until I can do a little rearranging of my own."

"You do realize," Jenny said, "that you and I are the only ones in L.A. that actually park our cars in the garage?"

"I'm sure there's at least one other person who does. Maybe we should find her and form a club."

As Jenny was untying the lid of her trunk to free the leather chair that protruded a foot from the end of the car, Diega said, "By the way, Erin wanted me to thank you for setting her up with the hospital."

"Any good news?" Jenny asked as she lifted the chair out of the trunk.

When Diega shook her head, Jenny put the chair on the driveway and leaned over to hug her friend. "I'm so sorry."

Once Jenny and Diega had the chair settled into Diega's garage, Jenny said, "I was talking to my law enforcement buddy, Ray. He told me that Mrs. Chambers got a ransom note for her son."

Diega decided it must be a day for surprises. "I really thought Wayne had run away."

"It gets better. The ransom was for fifty thousand. Small potatoes for that family. But guess who sent it?"

"I can only hope it was Carl. It would be nice to know he's off the streets."

"Nope." Jenny grinned. "Sonny boy, himself. The story he tells is that he was visiting a friend's house and parked his precious Harley on the street. When he came out, all that was left of his motorcycle was scrap metal. He figured it was a message from Carl or one of the other moneybags he contacted. Not being the brave sort, he decided that he'd better disappear and fast."

"And it costs money to disappear," Diega said.

"Right. So he and his friend concocted this fake kidnapping to raise the dough to get out of town."

"I wonder why he didn't just ask his mom for the money."

"Maybe he knew she wouldn't give it to him."

Diega leaned against her car. "Do you think his mama will send him out of the country for a while to keep him safe?"

Jenny snorted. "Last I heard she was considering pressing charges against him. Maybe she thinks he'll be safer in prison."

"And maybe," Diega said, "she doesn't care."

Chapter Twenty-nine

THE SUNSET STREAKED oranges and reds across feathery clouds as Diega sat in her art room absently shaping and remolding clay between her fingers as she gazed out the window. The room held labeled shelves with watercolor, acrylic, and oils paints, brushes, canvas, carving tools, and pottery tools. Inside the closet were more shelves, these designed for the slow drying of ceramic pieces that were in the leather stage.

Diega found her fingers shaping miniature people. A mother, a father, a daughter. A dead man. A wife by the body. A son astride a motorcycle. A teacher. Tiny, not fully formed shadow people all around the edges.

Stylized objects started to form. A poker table. A school. A home. A dollar sign. A bed. A key.

Diega could not discipline her mind. Instead of detailed lists of motives and timelines, her thoughts leapt from one person to another.

Who had a motive? Who had access to the school? Who else might be hiding in the background unnoticed?

Diega picked up the clay key and turned it over and over in her hand. That there was an essential piece of information missing, she did not doubt. She grappled with which area that particular key may fit.

Instead of crushing the figures back into one ball, Diega carried them to the drying racks and covered them loosely with plastic. Poirot she might not be, but she had a glimmer of the picture coalescing.

Diega sorted through her materials for the next day's lessons. She placed the pile by the back door so that she would not forget anything in the morning. As she mentally flipped a coin between reading and lazing in front of the television, the telephone rang.

Felicia sounded exhausted. "I was going to call you earlier, but I was on a roll. I finally finished packing my living room and most of the stuff that's going to storage. Maybe this move will really happen."

"We still on for Saturday at 8:00 a.m. at your place?"

"Just bring plenty of coffee and some doughnuts." A puff of air sounded over the receiver. "Anyway, speaking of murders, which we were not, I will give you my big news bulletin. My friend Mary who owns the salon that Mrs. Zeke goes to? Well, she called me to say that Mrs. Z brought an out-of-town friend in with her today and they were talking about money."

"Kind of a private thing to discuss in a public setting."

"Girlfriend, you would not believe what you overhear when cutting hair. I sometimes think holding a pair of scissors makes people assume you are deaf, dumb, and blind. Anyway, it seems we were wrong about the dead guy. He didn't have a pot to piss in."

"Zeke was broke? That can't be right. How in the world did he afford that kind of life?"

"Turns out it's Mrs. Chambers who has the money. She's a trust fund baby. Her great-great-granddaddy was one of the railroad barons who, depending on the source, either raped the lands in the early 1800s, or opened the West to progress. Doesn't much matter since he isn't around to stand trial nowadays." Felicia clicked her tongue in obvious disapproval. "Anyway, the misses was threatening to turn off the faucet of cash that Zeke boy made free and easy use of 'cause she had it on good faith that he was dirty dancing with some little chicky. If she found proof, she was going to chuck Zeke out on his sexy little bottom."

Diega chewed her bottom lip. She flipped through her mental pictures of the suspects in the case as if perusing a stack of baseball trading cards. Faces on the front, motives on the back. "Sounds like a good reason for Zeke to kill her, not for her to kill him. In fact, it takes away any motive for her to kill her hubby, unfaithful louse that he might have been."

"True enough. She who has the purse strings rules. No need to do anything crude like breaking your husband's skull open when you can have your social secretary pack his bags and leave them on the front porch."

IN THE LUNCHROOM the next day, Rita Morgan waved a stack of photos in her hand. "I finally got the pictures of the faculty Christmas party processed." She handed half the pile to Jim Tolkien and the other half to the teacher opposite him. "It took longer than I thought to finish the roll. I shot pictures of the squirrels in my backyard this weekend just to use up the film."

Jim passed each photo to Diega who, after dutiful examination, passed them along the line. Comments and laughter greeted each one.

The sixth picture caused Diega to stop and stare. The photograph showed several of the staff holding drinks and smiling against a backdrop of a Christmas tree and garlanded mantelpiece. But what caught Diega's attention was a beautiful French braid flowing down the back of one of the attendees.

Jim poked her as he handed her the stack that had piled up while she stared. Preoccupied, Diega flipped through the rest without seeing any of them. She suddenly realized that Felicia had handed her the key piece last night, and now motive, means, and opportunity all aligned. Keeping her eyes downcast, she hastily excused herself.

Diega rushed outside to the parking lot. Grateful that, for once, she had her cell phone with her, she huddled in the corner by the back wall while she dug for the business card that Detective Theophilus had given her. She pushed the number buttons as she started mentally reviewing salient facts, knowing she would have to do a lot of convincing to get the detective to act on her information.

"Theophilus here."

Diega identified herself. "I know who killed Zeke Chambers."

"Hang up," a voice from behind Diega commanded. "Now."

Diega felt a sharp jab to her head. She pushed a button and laid her phone on the block wall. "You make an even worse murderer than you do a teacher, Megan."

"I don't know. I've done pretty well so far." Megan Beaker came around to the side of Diega, a small, but lethal-looking gun wrapped in her hand. She was just out of Diega's reach.

Diega turned to fully face her. "If you shoot me out here in the parking lot, you'll never get away. People will hear. They'll come running. Even if you leave before they get here, someone is going to notice that you left the staff room right after I did."

"I'm not going to shoot you. You're going to commit suicide. I was going to set this up after school today, but when I saw you staring at those photos I knew you figured it out." She glanced at her watch, but not long enough for Diega to make any move. "There's fifteen minutes before the bell rings. You're going to leave a note saying how sorry you were for killing Zeke. That, along with the key and handkerchief I planted, will tidy things up and the police will finally leave."

Diega slowly inched away from the wall to give herself more room to maneuver. "You really should have stopped with Zeke's death. You could have pled involuntary manslaughter. I bet you didn't mean to kill him. You were the one he was waiting for in the hallway. And when you found him in my room bleeding after his fight with Sally's husband, you grabbed some paper towels and helped him. That's when you found out there wasn't any water in there, so you led him over to Rita's room. That's a lot of tenderness being shown, but, of course, it makes sense since you were his latest squeeze."

"I was not his 'squeeze.'" Megan's nostrils flared. "We weren't just lovers. Zeke and I were engaged. He was leaving his wife and we were going to get married."

Diega raised an eyebrow. "When did he tell you he wasn't leaving her after all?"

Megan's jaw jutted forward. "It's those stupid charter schools. He did everything he could to raise money for them. But it wasn't enough. He said he needed her money to make it happen. And she was getting suspicious about us. He actually said he wanted to stop seeing me." Megan's eyes widened, incredulous. "I told him the charter business wasn't important. We would be fine with our jobs. We could live on what we made. What was important was that we had each other."

Megan huddled against the hood of one of the cars, the gun still pointed at Diega. "He laughed. He actually laughed at me. He said I was an idiot to think he was going to give up his lifestyle to live some middle class existence with me. He turned his back on me. I looked around for something, anything, to throw at him, to hit him, to hurt him. The scissors were lying on the desk." Megan's eyes grew blank. She blinked and refocused on Diega. "I wiped off the scissors and my hands with his handkerchief. But I got a lot of blood on my sleeves. I knew I had to change my clothes. I left. That must have been when Luis saw me."

"He noticed that you were wearing different clothes?"

"He mentioned it to me later. I told him I had spilled paint on myself when I was preparing for class. But I knew he'd end up telling the police. I had to stop that."

"He didn't tell them, you know. He believed you. He didn't think twice about it."

"And I was supposed to gamble on that? Like I could trust you not to say anything either, right? You better dig out some paper and start writing. I'll even tell you what to say."

"Hey, Diega!" Diega's jogging buddy, Jack O'Reilly, and his two giant German Shepherds came loping up the street. The slightly smaller dog, Maggie, rushed to greet Diega while Abby, the bruiser, headed straight for Megan.

Megan shrieked, kicked at Abby, then swung the gun toward the gentle dog. Diega and Jack both screamed and lunged for Megan's arm. The gunshot exploded near Diega's ear, but the bullet flew harmlessly into the air. Megan twisted out of their grasps and Diega and Jack fell onto the pavement.

The school's side door burst open. "Freeze!" Detective Theophilus had his weapon drawn and pointed at Megan.

Megan sagged. Then her arm flew up, gun pointed at her temple.

Abby growled and leapt at Megan at the same time that Diega scrambled off the ground. They hit her together, knocking her to the asphalt. The gun fired again, but the bullet thudded into the side of a nearby car setting off its alarm. Before Megan could recover, Diega had her arms pinned. Abby stood guard, alternating between licking Diega's cheek and growling at Megan.

Theophilus locked handcuffs on Megan and hauled her to her feet. He nodded at the line of parked cars as he spoke to Diega. "You should have aimed her toward my car. Then the department would have to pay for a new paint job."

Chapter Thirty

"ZEKE NEEDED TO stay with his wife if he was to have access to the money he needed for the charter schools. That meant he had to get rid of any women he was fooling around with on the side. When I saw the photo of Megan wearing a braid, I thought of the description of Zeke's latest girlfriend. Then I remembered that Megan had a key that opened the cabinet in the auditorium—something only a master key could do—and it all clicked into place." Diega sighed and leaned back on the plastic chair. She and Detective Theophilus were alone in the teacher's lounge while crime scene investigators scoured the parking lot, and Megan was escorted to the police station by two uniformed officers.

"It was quick thinking to tell me where you were and smart of you to leave your speakerphone on. I was in Room Five when you called. I'm only sorry it took me a few minutes to find another phone and call for backup."

"I tried to stall her and give you time to get there. Thank God Jack decided to practice for the 10K around here and double thanks that he brought his sweet dogs with him."

"I'll have to bring his girls some doggy biscuits."

Diega picked up a paper napkin from the table and started folding it. "This whole situation has had one layer piled on top of the other. Zeke's drive for money makes me think of his son, Wayne. I hear he wrote himself his own ransom note."

Theophilus groaned. "That kid. First he stands outside that poker club and tries to loan people money—money he stole from his mother, by the way. The idiot doesn't have a clue about how to collect on these loans and before he can figure it out, Carl's goons come out and chase him off." A weary headshake. "So now that his kidnapping escapade has fallen apart, he's trying to get into the FBI witness program. Problem is, he didn't witness anything and is useless to them." He sighed, then tapped the table in front of Diega. "Speaking of Carl, we picked up one of his bodyguards. He stole the car that almost ran you down. We can charge him with car theft and reckless driving, but the D.A. doesn't think we can make a charge of attempted homicide stick. Sorry."

"I'm sorry you can't link it back to Carl. That man is scary."

"Sometimes we don't get all the bad guys. However, there's still hope with the Harrison Carter case. LAPD found the thugs who beat and dumped your teacher friend after he couldn't pay his debt to Carl. And one of those guys is talking. With some luck, Carl may end up wearing prison blues after all." Theophilus flipped his notebook closed.

He leaned forward and smiled at Diega, his eyes crinkling at the corners. "Now that you aren't officially involved in one of my cases, I was wondering if you'd like to have dinner sometime."

Diega felt the internal awkwardness that always arose for her in these situations. She sighed and returned his smile, but hers was rueful. "Truthfully, if I went for men, Detective Theophilus, you'd be the kind of guy I'd go for. But the fact of the matter is, I'm gay."

"Oh." Theophilus looked embarrassed. "Sorry. I guess I didn't read the signs very well." He slipped his notebook into his jacket pocket. He stood and stuck out his hand. "You really are a dynamic woman. Any more like you at home?"

Diega grabbed his hand and shook it. "As a matter of fact, there are. What are you doing Saturday afternoon? If you're free, I'd like to introduce you to my sister, Anita."

RAINBOW-COLORED PENNANTS snapped and rippled in the May breeze. Four women playing guitar, banjo, bass, and drums jammed on country songs of love and loss. Horses, awaiting their turn in the rodeo ring, neighed and grunted softly. The aroma of meats on the barbeque swept over everything, melding it into a whole.

Diega, beer in hand and a smile on her lips, absorbed every color, sound, and fragrance.

Tully, her hair now a vibrant red, nudged Diega with her elbow. "Right nice party. Reckon we did okay."

"I see your country girl persona is front and center today." Diega leaned into her friend, nodding at Felicia twirling Jenny through a complicated turn on the dance floor. "They're enjoying it. That's the important part."

"You look like you're enjoying it, too, good buddy. That's important to me." Tully dragged her friend over to two plastic chairs set in the shade of an oak tree. "I haven't had a chance to talk with Erin since her chemo ended. How's she doing?"

"Good." Diega spotted Erin immediately. Blue jeans, checked western shirt, boots, and a brown, felt cowboy hat covering her now-bald head, she stood in line to ride the mechanical bull. "The labs will be back Monday. Then we'll find out if the tumors shrank or not."

"Is she still thinking about the surgery?"

"If the cancer is contained and small enough, she'll have the mastectomy. If not..." Diega shrugged. She didn't have to continue.

Tully reached over and squeezed her knee.

"Surgery or no, we're heading for Europe for three weeks. Maybe in August."

"Who'll look after your furry children?"

"One of my nephews. He adores the cats and it seems mutual. Plus he's seventeen and eager to have a try at independence. Luckily, his folks live in South Pasadena, so I know he'll have backup."

"Give him my phone number, too." Tully thought for a moment, then added, "I'm sure my dad still has an apartment in Paris. You give me the dates and I'll bet he'll be glad to loan it to you. Might be a nice base of operations for you two."

"You're the best." Diega gave Tully a one-armed hug before pointing to the far corner of the field where the rodeo riders were setting up. A dark-haired young boy watched closely as they saddled the horses and checked their equipment. Gina Quinn stood by her son. When he turned to look up at her, Diega could see two profiles that shared a close genetic heritage. "I see David is quite avidly watching the riders. Does this mean there's a horse in his future?"

"I've taken him out riding a few times. It makes Gina nervous, but he's got a good seat. He's learning fast."

A breathless Felicia and Jenny collapsed on the grass at their feet.

Jenny laughed, "One more whirl around that dance floor and I'll need a nap before dinner."

"That can be arranged." Felicia patted her lap and Jenny laid her head on it. As she stroked Jenny's hair, Felicia looked up at Diega and said, "Erin tells me her mom is leaving Vista Elementary."

Diega nodded. "She's taking a job with Gwen running a charter school. Gwen was glad to have her ideas, and I think Sally is glad to be getting out of the GUSD." She stretched her legs and wiggled her toes inside her hiking boots. "Sally's not the only one jumping ship."

"Not you?" Jenny sounded shocked.

"No. At least not yet. Jim's proposal for a charter elementary school made it through the preliminary round and is going to be considered by the Board in June. Even if it's approved, the school wouldn't open until the Fall of 2000, so it's a ways before I have to decide if I'm going with him."

"The millenium." Felicia's voice held a tinge of awe. "I wonder if it's going to be a magical time or just another year."

Diega's eyes swept over her friends and then rested on Erin, the brightest point for her in the entire crowd. Erin looked over at that moment and waved to Diega, then climbed aboard the bull. "I really don't know about the future. I'm learning to enjoy each day as it comes."

Other Jane DiLucchio titles you may enjoy:

Relationships Can Be Murder

Relationships Can Be Murder. That's what Diega DelValle concludes when she finds herself alienated from her lover because of her affair with Sheila Shelbourne, Los Angeles TV newscaster and woman-about-town. Diega's woes only increase when Sheila is found beaten to death and the police focus their investigations upon her.

Diega summons help from her three best buddies, Tully, Felicia, and Jenny. Together they delve into the world of television where they encounter an arena where ratings can be a matter of life and death. There's Rachel who was vying with Sheila for a New York job. Or was she? Her husband Curtis maintains Rachel would kill for Sheila's now open position in L.A. But then Curtis has his own, very old, axe to grind with Sheila. Has their past relationship caused her demise?

Then again, Sheila's ex-husband is in the picture as well. Newly arrived from San Diego and famous for hurling items at Sheila's women, does Steve have his own murderous thoughts about Sheila? Aurora thinks so. However, as Sheila's discarded lover, Aurora may have her own agenda.

Family relationships are also suspect. Henry and Francine Shelbourne had two daughters, Sheila and Natalie. Both daughters are now dead. Coincidence? Or did the secret that bound the sisters together bring both their deaths years apart?

In the midst of trying to clear Diega, the four women discover that one of them has an even better motive than Diega for wanting Sheila dead—a discovery that drives a wedge between the friends. In the meantime, new relationships develop and get in the way of their investigation. The ever-amorous Tully finds herself drawn to the enticing police detective and Felicia and Jenny are discovering each other's charms. No one but Diega seems to realize that Relationships Can Be Murder. Then Diega, herself, becomes the target. Is she the victim of one of her own relationships or is she getting too close to the truth?

Available in eBook Formats only

eISBN: 978-1-61929-241-3

Vacations Can Be Murder

When her friends take Diega DelValle on an impromptu vacation to Talkeetna, Alaska, they envision a quiet setting in which to give Diega a breather from both teaching and heartbreak. However, even before the friends arrive, this small town on the edge of Denali National Park becomes a less than idyllic vacation spot. Gail, a Talkeetna native, dies on the mountain. Melissa, Gail's cousin and a former student of Diega's, arrives in Talkeetna and raises doubts about the death being accidental. Due to Melissa's pleas for help, Diega and her friends are thrust into an investigation of a small town and its inhabitants-an unsavory pastime that turns deadly.

Coming in June 2016

Going Coastal

A client dying on her massage table is traumatic enough for Kate Matthews, but when the police declare that death a murder, life becomes more painful for her as she is cast as the major suspect.

None of this is what Kate expected from her move to the peaceful town of Santa Barbara. After a near-fatal heart attack, an early retirement from her Los Angeles law firm, and a change in careers, Kate envisioned a quiet life with her wife, Alicia, and their grown children.

Since the client held a position on the California Coastal Commission, her death becomes a media event. Kate finds herself and her family sucked into the maelstrom. The former lawyer has all she can do to find the truth behind Celia's death without adding her own name to the body count.

Coming in February 2016

Other Quest Books you may enjoy:

Ten Little Lesbians
by Kate McLachlan

Ten women, guests at the lesbian-owned Adelheid Inn, are stranded in the Cascade Mountains after a mudslide closes the only road out. One goes missing. One is killed. More than one is not who she pretends to be, and every one of them has a secret. When another woman is attacked, it become clear there's a killer in their midst, and it has to be one of them.

Is it Beatrice, the judge, surly and sad after the death of her long-term partner? Or her niece, Tish, angry and sullen at being kept under Beatrice's thumb? Or is it Carmen, Beatrice's childhood friend who lured her to the Inn under false pretenses?

It couldn't be the Mormon girls, Amy and Dakota. Or could it? Perhaps it's Paula, the gallant butch, or her date, the lovely and silent Veronica. A blind woman couldn't do it, but is Jess really blind? And what about Holly, the hotel manager who is just a bit too perky, or Lila, the mysterious owner of the hotel?

One thing quickly becomes clear. They'd better find out, before there are none.

ISBN: 978-1-61929-236-9
eISBN: 978-1-61929-235-2

Illusive Witness
by S.Y. Thompson

Who can you turn to when everyone betrays your trust? This is an especially important question for Ruth Gallagher. Severely injured at the same time that her best friend is killed in a mountain climbing incident, she later learns it was no accident. Repeated attempts on her life are made when a mobster believes she knows more about his criminal enterprises than she does.

Riding to the rescue is U.S. Marshal Emma Blake, but after all the perfidy can Ruth trust Emma? Barely healed from her previous encounters, she may not have a choice.

ISBN: 978-1-61929-234-5
eISBN: 978-1-61929-233-8

White Roses Calling
by Dakota Hudson

Sydney Rutledge is a rising star in the Los Angeles District Attorney's Office. In the midst of a career making serial murder prosecution she finds herself having an unexpected attraction to the arresting officer in the case—a female police sergeant. The attraction leads her to a confusing journey of self-discovery in regards to her own sexuality.

Sergeant Alex Chambers is a talented veteran of the LAPD. Fearless on the streets but gun shy when it comes to relationships—the result of a heartbreak years prior. Despite this she cannot deny the attraction she is feeling towards a certain beautiful—and straight—assistant district attorney.

As the women attempt to figure out their emerging relationship, a serial murderer begins targeting female attorneys in the southland. The killings appear to be a copy cat of the case which introduced the two, yet that killer remains behind bars. When it becomes apparent the killer has set his sights on Sydney, Alex vows to protect her—even at the potential cost of her own life.

ISBN: 978-1-61929-170-6
eISBN: 978-1-61929-171-3

No Thru Road
by Linda M. Vogt

Newspaper reporter Riley Logan is looking forward to a peaceful week when she goes with her best friend Marie to beautiful Galiano Island, B.C. Instead, the two find themselves in the middle of an environmental clash, a decades-old mystery and the murder of a well-loved islander. The women stay at the Cliffhouse, a funky waterfront cottage Riley has inherited from her aunt, where they discover 60-year-old letters that may hold important clues. And then strange things start happening on Galiano... a ferry rams the dock, an oil slick coats the harbor and Riley's new love interest, Kit, disappears and is named a suspect in the murder. Will Riley and Marie use her aunt's letters to solve the murder? What did someone hide on nearby Wallace Island that could break the case open? And what happened to Kit? The answers to those questions, along with love, adventure and a dash of humor, can be found in Linda M. Vogt's debut novel.

ISBN: 978-1-61929-212-3
eISBN: 978-1-61929-211-6

OTHER REGAL CREST PUBLICATIONS

Be sure to check out our other imprints,
Mystic Books, Quest Books, Silver Dragon Books,
Troubadour Books, Young Adult Books, and Blue Beacon Books.

About the Author

Jane DiLucchio, a retired professor at a community college with a previous incarnation as an elementary school teacher, enjoys reading, cards games, theater-going, amateur farming, travel, food, wine, friends, and laughter. Jane, her wife, and their two furry children make their home in southern California.

VISIT US ONLINE AT
www.regalcrest.biz

At the Regal Crest Website You'll Find

- The latest news about forthcoming titles and new releases

- Our complete backlist of romance, mystery, thriller and adventure titles

- Information about your favorite authors

- Current bestsellers

- Media tearsheets to print and take with you when you shop

- Which books are also available as eBooks.

Regal Crest print titles are available from all progressive booksellers including numerous sources online. Our distributors are Bella Distribution and Ingram.

CPSIA information can be obtained at www.ICGtesting.com
Printed in the USA
LVOW06s1912011115

460628LV00001B/31/P